CRAB ATTACK!

MICHAEL COLE

SEVEREDPRESS

CRAB ATTACK

Copyright © 2022 by Michael Cole

WWW.SEVEREDPRESS.COM

ISBN: 978-1-922861-41-2

CHAPTER 1

"You hear that?"

Larry Henn made the mistake of turning to the sound of his brother's voice. "What is it this time?"

"Listen…" Timothy Henn looked to the trees, holding his hand out as though to point at whatever he thought lurked in the darkness.

Two seconds into the silence, and Larry was already fed up. He just wanted to fish, smoke, and eat a bunch of high-sodium junk food which he couldn't touch at home. For the sake of argument, he listened. All he could hear were frogs, crickets, cicadas, crackling of fire, and the mild lapping of water. The only sound he *wanted* to hear was the strain on his rod.

"There's nothing out there." He planted his pipe between his teeth and faced the water. The moonlight reflected perfectly off the lake, giving the trees across from him a haunting quality. Better yet, there was not a single cloud in the sky, granting him a picture-perfect view of the stars and moon. It couldn't get much better than this. All it would take was for Timothy's excessive worrying to vanish.

The forty-one year old accountant finally sat in his wicker chair, his eyes fixed on the shoreline further down. The cattails and weed beds were thicker down there, as were the grouping of trees on the shoreline.

"Could've sworn I heard something."

"Every time," Larry said. "It's the woods. Things live in it. Squirrels, raccoons… After thirty-something years, I *still* have to explain this to you?"

"It wasn't a raccoon, dude," Timothy said. "It was big. Big enough to break some branches."

Larry watched his tobacco pipe dangling from his lips. It used to belong to his father until he passed away from brain cancer two years ago. Medical records going back ten generations showed no history of cancer. Dad managed to be the unlucky one to break that streak. While the poor guy was

1

still lucid, he gifted it to Larry, who treasured the item as well as the memories that came with it. Many of those memories involved camping here at Lake Lucas, a vast stretch of water in the Midwest, home to numerous species of fish.

Dad was gone, as was his older brother Brandon, thanks to an incompetent taxi driver in New Jersey. Mom had passed in '03 after literally getting struck by lightning. Arrived late from the coffee shop where she managed. A big storm was blowing through. She was halfway from the car to the door when *FLASH!* There was no scream, no dramatic spasm. Her life had disappeared as quickly as the bolt that struck her.

Fate had not been kind to this generation of the Henn family—the 'Henn House' as they jokingly called it. At least once a year, they would have a camping trip here at Lake Lucas. Everyone had their own tent. Dad would spend most of his time fishing and smoking. Mom spent much of her time reading books. Sometimes the brothers would kayak, play sports or board games, among other things to pass the time.

Now, it was just Larry and Timothy. While Larry loved coming here, it was a bit of a chore to bring his brother along. Had they not been the only ones left, he would probably not bother with these 'family trips'. However, Larry was a believer in Heaven, and he couldn't shake the feeling that Mom and Dad were keeping an eye on him. Maybe if his wife and kids were the sort that enjoyed camping, he could get away with not inviting Timothy. He tried once. Jessica and the boys *hated* it— as in they spent the entire five days complaining nonstop. At that point, it became clear that camping was something he would either enjoy alone, or in his brother's company.

The former was starting to feel a bit more appealing.

A tug on his line triggered the pleasure centers in his brain. Larry set the hook and started cranking. Right away, he knew it was a panfish. All credit given where it was due, the fella gave it his best fight, but he lacked the power that the smallmouths contained.

Larry raised the line and let the fish dangle. A bluegill, roughly nine inches long. Nothing wrong with a good panfish, especially with beer batter coating. He unhooked his victim and tossed it in the bucket. Tomorrow, it would meet its demise at the point of his filleting knife.

"Want a beer?" Timothy asked.

"Nah. I'd rather go for a coffee, to be honest."

"That doesn't sound bad, actually. I'm not even close to feeling drowsy, anyway. I guess I'll get to brewing some up." Timothy went to work filling the kettle with water, then put it over the fire.

Larry was simply grateful he didn't have to get up. Maybe bringing Timothy on these trips wasn't so bad after all. He baited his hook, then tossed a cast sixty-feet out. Taking a puff on his pipe, he leaned back, feet crossed a few inches from the waterline.

"What the…"

Larry groaned. "Now what?"

"I heard something again," Timothy said.

"That was my bait hitting the water."

"No… over there."

Larry looked up the shore a ways. This time, he could hear the movement in the cattails. He shrugged, then focused on his line. "Probably just a bear."

"A bear?"

"Come on, Tim. You know this. Bears aren't gonna wander over to camp, especially if there's a fire."

The rustling continued for a few moments. Next was a sound of lapping water. Whatever had cut through the vegetation had moved into the lake. That had Larry's attention. Animals on land was par for the course, but he couldn't think of anything that would wander far out into the water like that.

Squinting, he could almost see a shape in the distance. The moonlight provided just enough visibility that he could make out the presence of something fairly large. His mind's eye was convinced it was a buck. Made sense. Once in a while, they'd venture out into the water. Though, he could swear the thing had a weird shape, like that of a hockey puck.

Curiosity finally got the better of him. He stood up and leaned over the water for a better look. *Damn!* It was gone. His eyes backtracked over the direction it came. No movement, no sounds of splashing or bending cattails. Looking at the water, he noticed a few tiny swells.

Did it submerge?

"I don't hear anything anymore," Timothy said.

"No shit, Sherlock. The thing went out and…" He stopped himself, believing his description would unnerve his jittery brother further. "I think it swam off."

"Wait, swam off?"

"Yes. Animals can swim. What's got you all freaked out?"

"I don't know… Well, you know…"

Larry shook his head. "No."

"Just last week, that guy disappeared on the south end of the lake. They never found him…"

"Oh him? Didn't his fiancée dump him? Got depressed and went to his family cabin?" Larry cranked his reel, then drew from his pipe. "Probably hung himself somewhere in the woods."

"They would've found him," Timothy said. "Maybe we should've held this trip off until they've ruled out any… you know… foul play."

Larry snorted. "What? You think there's some guy with a hockey mask and a machete wandering around out here?"

"No, but something's off about that story. One of the articles said that the plank on the end of his pier was splintered, like a big pickaxe had come down on it. His fishing pole was found in the shallows nearby…"

"Dude, I'm starting to think drinking coffee might not be in your best interest tonight. The cops didn't find anything, in the water, nor in the woods. Maybe the guy hooked up with some broad and moved to California. Bottom line, stop pissing yourself. And by the way, how's that coffee coming?"

Timothy checked the kettle. "Aw, hell."

Larry shook his head. *Dummy let it go for too long.* If the water got too hot, it would extract too much flavor from the coffee grounds. He had heard Vietnam vets brag about this bitter flavor, but Larry was a mere civilian with too much of a sheltered life. Camping in a tent and making cowboy coffee was the closet he would ever come to being an outdoorsman. That, and shore dinners.

Timothy refilled the kettle and set it up again, checking his watch to mark the time. Two minutes should do it.

Larry's line went taut. The pole bent, threatening to fly from his hands.

"Whoa!" He stood up.

4

Timothy approached the water. "Got something?"

"Nah. My bait's just trying to escape!" Larry retorted.

Timothy bit his lip, his way of admitting it was a dumb question. He stood at the shoreline and watched his brother struggle against the unseen foe. His anxiety transformed into a childlike excitement when he saw the fish brush the surface.

"There it is!"

"Yep. A pike!" Larry's enthusiasm equaled his brother's. Not only had he not hooked one of these bad boys in years, he was amazed he got it on a crawler harness. Typically, they preferred to go for spinner baits or minnows. But it was not out of the realm of possibility.

He smiled, thinking of the time his dad hooked a thirty-six inch pike with a fly rod. If only the guy could be here to witness this. Larry only got a brief glimpse, but it was enough to see that this catch was around forty inches.

It tried to run with his line. Only by pure luck was he still bringing it in. The teeth on a pike were more than enough to sever the line. The thing just needed to clamp down hard enough.

Don't you dare... "AH SHIT!" In the blink of an eye, the line went slack. Timothy chuckled at his brother's expense.

"Oh, man! What a burn!"

"Aw, shut up."

Timothy's laugh intensified. "I'll have to tell Jessica about your little misfortune. She always appreciates a good laugh at your expense."

"Oh yeah? How 'bout I tell her about you pissing your pants over ghost stories. 'Oh, something's moving in the woods. I need my teddy bear.' 'Help me! I think there's something in the water! I'm so scared.'"

Timothy looked away and smirked. His brother's mockery was successful in making him feel foolish for displaying such timidness. Yeah, his sister-in-law would get a laugh out of this little camping story. That smile widened. For now, *he* would get a laugh out of Larry's misfortune.

"You still lost a pike. You know, I remember being out with dad, and we saw a little seven year old girl reel one in. Guess she's more the angler than the great Larry Henn!"

Larry stepped back, eyebrows raised. "Oh, I see how it is, you little shit." He squinted, now looking behind Timothy into the water. "Oh, SHIT! Tim, I think you were right. I think I see someone moving on the shore across from us."

Timothy's amusement turned to alarm. He spun on his heel to look, cupping one hand over his eyes as he scoured the water, while grabbing his car keys with the other. There was nothing but water and moonlight reflection.

"Where? I don't see..." Larry shoved him into the water. Timothy fell forward, his cursing drowned out by the lake. He emerged, waist deep in water, glaring at his older brother who stood cackling from the shore. "You jackass!"

Larry was doubled over, unable to contain himself. "B— Better get out, Tim! There might be a bloodthirsty killer in that lake! Don't wanna get hacked to bits!"

Timothy raised a middle finger. "I'm gonna kill you."

"Aw, you all wet? Hope you packed some spare clothes." Larry sucked in a deep breath in an attempt to control himself. Bringing Timothy along was officially worth it now just for this moment alone.

"Damn you. You made me drop my keys."

"You know, I'd feel bad, but seeing you getting ready to haul ass out of here made it even better."

"Won't be so funny if we can't drive out of here." Timothy put his face to the water. "Great! I can't see a damn thing!"

"Dig around. Might have to get low, though."

"I'm gonna kill you," Timothy said, much to his brother's amusement. "You're buying me a new fob when we get home."

"Fine."

"And are you gonna reel that thing in? Or are you gonna risk letting me get hooked by your lure?"

Larry blew a raspberry, then started cranking. "Oh, please! The pike bit through. There's nothing at the end of..." He looked where the line touched the water. There was weight at the end. Not a lot, but enough to create drag.

Plop!

Larry looked to his brother. Arms and legs thrashed in a pool of frothing water. "Dude? Did you seriously fall?"

He saw Timothy's feet kicking. A hand reached high, fingers outstretched and curling repeatedly in a grabbing motion.

Larry chuckled. "Not working, buddy. I'm not gonna fall for it. Go ahead and pretend like your being hacked to death by some underwater—" Larry brought the lure out of the water. Dangling from the lure was the head of his pike, severed at the gill slits. Swaying back and forth, it hung slack-jawed, eyes staring into the black night. Larry touched the head and examined the stump. A clean cut, the edges slightly compressed, as though squeezed first. As though a giant pair of dull scissors closed over it. "—predator…"

Tim broke the surface. Larry could do nothing but shriek. Both of his brother's arms had been severed above the elbow. Timothy screamed, the two stumps spurting blood to his left and right.

His assailant emerged directly behind him. Moonlight glinted off of its disk-shaped body. Two edged appendages, like massive sheers, lashed at him. They pierced Timothy's back like javelins. He tried to yell, but all that came out was a raspy gasp, for all the air was instantly removed from his lungs.

Timothy disappeared under a wave of red water. The thing was on him, eight legs protruding from its sides. The claws dug into their prize, ripping fabric and flesh.

"Sweet Mary, mother of everything good and holy…"

The bending of cattails and the crushing of twigs made Larry look to the north. From the woods emerged another predator, even larger than the one that took down Timothy. It spotted the frightened human, then darted on eight legs, claws outstretched.

Larry backed up, dropping the rod. *A spider. A fucking spider…* The claws snipped the air, determined to find flesh. *No… a CRAB!*

Lightning. A taxi. Brain cancer. The rest of his family got off lucky, for his unlikely demise was to be torn apart by a monster crustacean.

Those claws reached their target. Larry floundered in the mud, his midsection flayed open. Entrails were yanked free. Snippers worked their way up his torso, sawing through ribs, stomach, and lungs.

The crabs let nothing go to waste. Meat, bone, hair, even some of the fabric served as food.

Once they were done, they returned to the water, their hunger momentarily satisfied. The others which lay submerged in the weed beds, not so much. They would have to wait for other unsuspecting prey to approach the water's edge.

CHAPTER 2

"Gosh, it's an entire circus."

Deputy Taylor Davies barely registered her partner's commentary. It was one of those days where she regretted hitting the gym before work. For whatever reason, she could not stay asleep last night. Looking at the clock and seeing it was 4:00 a.m., she figured she may as well go. Laying in bed staring at the ceiling was doing her no good. Sixty minutes of cardio and thirty minutes of weightlifting followed, at the end of which, her mind abruptly decided it was ready for rest. Too late. 7:00 a.m. was around the corner, and her uniform was back at home waiting.

Now, she was struggling to get through the day. Her first cup of coffee failed to do anything, except go straight to her bladder. Despite this, she still went for a second and third.

Just one of those days.

All she could do was wait out the shift and hope nothing drastic came up. Currently, that waiting was spent in the driver's seat of her patrol car, watching the line of vehicles passing through the intersection. They were all going to the same destination: the Arthur Bowen property on the north end of Lake Lucas. The traffic lights turned to red, with four vehicles still on approach. The closest one to the light gunned the accelerator, shooting his red sportscar through the intersection two seconds after the light changed.

Deputy Alan Goldstein leaned forward, his own coffee swishing at the rim of his cup. "You see that?"

Taylor looked at him, her eyes shifting to the black drops running down the length of his cup. "You see *that*?"

He looked down, then rolled his eyes. "Cry me a river."

"Put the cover back on. I'm not interested in listening to Second Shift bitch about coffee stains again."

Alan begrudgingly pressed the cover onto his cup, then tilted his head toward the road.

"We gonna do something about that? They ran a red right in front of us?"

"Nope."

"Seriously?"

"Unless these people murder somebody, I'm not subjecting myself to the headache. This is Arthur Bowen's party. That hotshot in the red Dodge Viper... that's his soon-to-be son-in-law."

Alan shrugged, his face a haze of disapproval. "So what?"

"So, I just want to get through the next couple of days," Taylor said. "Mr. Bowen's daughter is getting married on Saturday. The people in his family are entitled, and frankly, quite nuts. We ticket any of these morons, we risk turning the entire group into an angry mob. I'm not kidding. We'd be lucky if they only flood our office with calls. Doesn't matter how legit our actions are. Call me lazy if you want to, but I'm not interested in the headache."

She rested against the headrest and watched the traffic gradually go by. The intersecting light changed to yellow, the remaining parties moments from continuing their course.

In the oncoming lane, a white Ford F-150 approached. It stopped several yards short of the intersection and made a turn into a nearby shop. As soon as the light turned green, the first vehicle in the line went from zero to seventy miles-per-hour. It raced through the intersection and the next thirty feet of lane, only to hit its brakes and swerve to avoid hitting the truck. The spoiled driver blared his horn, yelling something out the window before racing up the road to catch up with the others.

The Ford F-150 made its way into the parking lot, settled in a space, its driver stepping out with a glare on his face.

Taylor recognized the short-sleeve denim shirt, mud-stained work boots and jeans, and the black Miami Marlins ball cap. Valentine Krane, a nice looking man somewhere in his mid-thirties, turned his eyes to the parked police SUV across the road. The way he shrugged 'whatever', then grinned, indicated he recognized her through the open window.

She shrugged, then grinned. Valentine, known to most simply as Val, was pretty good at shrugging off such incidents. Ever since he moved into town, he kept to his contracting business, which he started with some money passed down from his late uncle. The only reason this information got out was due to the uncle's nosey caretaker, who couldn't keep a secret to save her life.

"You know where Thomas Krane's savings account is going? His nephew... you know? The EX-CON nephew. Guess even after robbing a bank, you can still get rewarded with six figures and a house on the lake. Yeah, he left the property to him too."

It didn't take long for that to go through the town. Taylor resented busybodies, especially ones that did not get the facts right. As she later learned, Val was, in fact, not getting six figures as the home aid claimed, but twenty grand. Not a bad gift, but nowhere near the riches that were rumored. Still, the yapping opened the floodgates, with a few jealous types complaining about Valentine Krane's criminal past.

These types included Deputy Alan Goldstein, as displayed in his next statement.

"Ah, there's the felon."

Taylor groaned. Feeling drowsy, it wasn't hard for her partner's whining to grate on her nerves. She had no sympathy for active criminals. Those who served their time and legitimately wanted to move on, however, that was a different story. Val was no murderer, rapist, or pedophile. From what she saw in his records, he plead guilty for armed robbery and a separate count of battery—which was what got him arrested in the first place.

Obviously, not a great thing to have on one's record, but context matters. The guy he got in a fight with was someone he caught screwing his then-girlfriend. Not an excuse, but still, context—he didn't pull some random person off the sidewalk and start clubbing at him.

It was that context that made Taylor somewhat sympathetic regarding the battery. Five years ago, she walked into the exact same scenario. She and her partner at the time stopped by her house around lunch so Taylor could grab a sandwich she left in the fridge. Lo and behold, right there on the couch was her live-in boyfriend and the clerk from the shop he worked at, naked as the day God made them.

Had it not been for her partner holding her back, *Taylor* would've been the one charged with aggravated battery—if not something worse.

The armed-robbery was plain foolishness, though a weapon was never pointed, but insinuated. By protocol, bank tellers are supposed to give the cash over and not call the robber's bluff.

Valentine Krane's crimes were paid with six years in prison. He was thirty-one years old when he was released. It seemed the guy was on the straight and narrow now. Not even a traffic violation. Taylor remembered having organized debates in college regarding society's treatment of ex-cons. Do they deserve eternal judgement, even after their sentence was served? Some thought it depended on the damages done, and Taylor usually found herself in that crowd. Nobody was hurt at the bank—there wasn't even a dramatic scene. He had simply gone to the counter and slipped the teller a note. The only guy hurt was an in-the-moment crime of passion. It did not make it right, but it at least made it different, considering he had no other record of assault, even in prison. That was Taylor's opinion, which was often maligned by her fellow deputies.

Who knows? Maybe I'm wrong. After all, the best way to avoid the scrutiny is to not commit the stupid crime in the first place.

"Wish I had an uncle to leave me a bunch of money to start a business."

Once again, Taylor's nerves were grated. "What would you prefer he did with it? Cocaine? Hookers?"

As usual, Alan did not have an answer for that. Maybe it was part of being a macho deputy, or maybe he held a personal grudge against ex-cons. Regardless, Taylor thought his attitude was indicative of the fact that criminals never truly pay their debt to society.

Several minutes later, they saw Val step out of the hardware store with supplies in hand. He gave the deputies a wave, then got in his car and pulled out onto the road, this time without the hindrance of speeding traffic.

Alan did a mock wave. "Yeah, yeah. Go about your day."

Taylor shot him a look. "You really have a hard-on for that guy, don't you?"

"Apparently, *you* do."

"Ah, yes. I stand up for him, therefor I must want to screw him. Great logic."

Alan chuckled. "I've seen enough women who proved that sentiment right."

"Good God." Taylor rubbed her head. As she feared, a migraine was emerging, no thanks to her partner's aggravation. Further souring her mood was her coffee. She took a sip, tasted the bitter cold beverage, then spat it out the window.

"Oh, and you complain about *me* making a mess?!" Alan said, pointing at the drips of coffee on the inner door.

"Shut up."

Taylor wiped the mess up with her napkin, then looked at the clock. Time was not moving. At this point, she was desperate. She reached for the radio knob and turned on the local news. As far as she was concerned, anything was better than Alan's obnoxious observations.

"*...efforts are on the way. The manager of the Dycan-Eclipse Nuclear Power Plant had made his second public statement, after it was discovered that radioactive materials had been improperly and illegally disposed in Lake Alocasia. Several tests have revealed massive radiation spikes in the water and its fish populations, sparking concerns that everything in the lake might have to be put down.*

"*Efforts to clean up the disaster are now resuming after the strange disappearance of the Shenkarow family, who mysteriously disappeared while camping near one of the coves.*"

Taylor turned the knob. The next station was playing rap music. *I'd rather have the headache.* She changed the channel again, this time finding another news station.

Alan rested his head on his palm, watching her sort through the stations. "Does your phone not work?"

"Never gets a signal when we're anywhere near the lake." He held up his phone. "Mine does!"

"Congratulations."

Alan reached over and switched the radio off. "Come on. Let's drive around. Beats sitting here staring at the hardware store." He scrolled through his phone. "I'll put on a podcast. Fill the dead silence."

Finally, something Taylor could agree with. She started the patrol vehicle and drove onto the road.

CHAPTER 3

It's her big day.

That was what Arthur Bowen continuously reminded himself whenever a new ping of stress hit him. He wasn't a big fan of weddings to begin with, not even his own. It always amounted to a party which cost more than it was worth, catering over sixty people, most of whom he didn't know—or care to know. Back when it was his turn, he simply wanted to go to the courthouse and get it over with. Mrs. Bowen had other plans, however. Like many women, she had big dreams of the perfect wedding. As far as he saw it, it was her big day.

The two-story lakefront property overlooked the north end of the lake. Arthur had purchased it after winning his first big settlement. It was against the CEO of a car dealership. It was always said that car salesmen should never be trusted, but not in the way his client figured. The defendant had initially denied the sexual assault allegation by her, and simply figured he would outspend her in court.

Lucky for the plaintiff, she had a lawyer with an attitude. An attitude, and a few connections. A few under-the-counter dealings led to 'accidentally' leaked recordings and images of prior incidents. As it turned out, this CEO had quite the history, and had done a decent job of covering things up until that point. He had a lot on the line, and his accuser's lawyer was not going to let up. Not wanting this debacle to get into the public eye, he arranged for 'negotiations'.

A few private meetings were held.

The judge did not ask why the charges were dropped. With the client being a nobody, the public did not enquire about the sudden increase in her net worth. Not all victories were won in the courtroom. As long as Arthur got a cut of the bribe—*settlement*—he didn't mind. It was a case where everyone won. The CEO kept his name clear, the client got a significant payoff, twenty-percent of which went to her lawyer.

It was enough to open his own firm. Business expanded, settlements were reached. Lawsuits, divorces, there was always somebody suing somebody. Each one added to the stuffing in Arthur Bowen's pocket.

Wealth brought power, and power quickly got to his head, though not nearly to the extent as his wife and daughter's. There was something about marrying into or being born into money that spawned entitlement. Arthur worked for it, regardless of the ethics involved, or lack thereof. He cherished his wealth, and even as it climbed, felt that it could always be lost at a moment's notice. He always kept an eye on the books, monitoring every dollar that came and went.

Wanda and Leslie, on the other hand, simply saw an endless stream of funds, evidenced by their behaviors on the lawn.

Arthur stood on the back porch, silently groaning as he watched hordes of people moving about on the grass. He always viewed this property as his private refuge, somewhere to get away from the rest of the world. His daily life was full of interactions, and he needed somewhere to enjoy his solitude. The fact that these people were helping to set up the party made no difference to that mindset.

His daughter Leslie was at the bottom of the hill, looking out at Lake Lucas. Since entering college, she always had the short shorts, midriff look. It probably was what caught the eye of her fiancé Dale Woods. It certainly caught the attention of other boys—her looks, and her father's bank account. At least Dale had his own business, which was steadily expanding. It was the winning factor that made Arthur comfortable enough to approve this arrangement. No way was he going to fund some everyday jackass expecting daddy-in-law to buy him a new car every year.

Her bridesmaids were with her, chatting about whatever young ladies talked about. Arthur didn't even know most of them. The only one whose name he remembered was Robin Berry, only because she had the most baggage. Boyfriend issues, usually. Go figure the prick was going to be a groomsman for Dale.

Midway up the hill was another annoyance, one that could not be missed—by sight or sound. His wife—or as Arthur thought, the woman who *ate* his wife—was on her phone. After over two decades of marriage, she was a far cry from the woman he married. Often, Arthur thought of the day he and Wanda first hooked up.

Oh, how smoking hot she was back then. Tan, tone, hair down, great yabbos.

Watching her, he couldn't help but wince as though in physical pain. Everything he liked was still there, somewhere.

Yeah, still there. Under several layers.

Wanda Bowen strutted back and forth, nearly yelling into her phone. On the line was a clerk from some flower company. Arthur was not the most empathetic of individuals, but even he felt pity for the poor guy. Or gal—Wanda had used the word 'bitch' at least once. Guy or gal, at least someone could now relate to the misery he lived with.

"No, *Saturday.* Not Sunday. Not Friday. Not today. *Saturday,* you dumb bitch… Don't give me attitude, just fulfill the order as planned… This is *not* last minute, I first got in touch with you yesterday… What difference does it make the amount of lilies I'm ordering?... You know what? Fuck yourself. And while you do, I'll be making a few calls regarding your business. Have fun watching your clientele go elsewhere." She hung up. "Stupid bitch. Looks like a job for the gang."

Arthur's resentment climbed. The 'gang' were several journalist friends she became acquainted with over the years. On the local and state level, they had grown to be fairly influential. 'A job for the gang' meant forking over money to draw customers away from a business.

More money out of my pocket.

Wanda was back on the phone, this time with a different flower company. "Yes, I'd like to place an order. Two-hundred lilies, fifty sunflowers, and… you know what? Throw in a hundred roses while you're at it… We need the delivery by Saturday morning… nine o'clock." She looked to the sky and groaned. "…you're not open until eleven?!... the wedding's at ten-thirty! We need the flowers… Yes, I heard you the first time. Not open till eleven. What, you think I'm deaf?..." Another groan. "Is the owner there?... Let me speak with him…" She paced for a few moments until the owner was on the line. "Yes, hi… Yeah, eleven is too late. We won't have time to set the flowers up properly… yeah I know you think it's last minute, but the last deal we had fell through... Tell you what, it's my daughter's wedding. I'll throw in a two-thousand dollar bonus if the flowers are here by nine."

A smile came over her pudgy face. The deal was obviously accepted.

Arthur looked to his coffee, then to one of the butlers he had hired. "Take this. Bring me a morning mimosa, with a fresh orange slice. I'm gonna need it."

"Yes sir." The server disappeared into the house.

Servers... another expense out of his pocket. But it was Wanda and Leslie's insistence that they live large these next few days.

It's her big day. Just get through it.

Wanda hung up the phone and looked to her husband, her mood enhanced exponentially. "Got the flower situation taken care of!"

Arthur snorted. She said that as though she expected him to care. After twenty-four years, he should not have expected anything different. The one who did care was Leslie. She broke away from her bridesmaids, joining her mother in celebration.

Arthur turned to the butler and took the freshly mixed drink, then tilted his head at the women. "You'd think they defeated Putin."

The butler smiled. "Yes sir." He disappeared back into the house, leaving his boss alone on the porch to drink his sorrows away.

That he did. The lawyer tilted the glass and downed half its contents. The next few minutes were wasted overseeing the disfigurement of his precious lawn. At the base of the hill, a canopy was being set up. It stretched the thirty feet between the hill and the dock. Chairs were being set up inside, as well as a booth for the candles and all the other nonsense that wedding couples put themselves through.

At the top of the hill, a DJ station was being assembled. The mere sight of that guy made Arthur finish his glass and call the butler back for a refill. This DJ cost as much as the catering, and he had not even heard of the guy until now. He even forgot the guy's name two minutes after he was introduced.

Horse? Mustang? QUARTER HORSE!

Arthur needed more alcohol. Quarter horse for a DJ name? It didn't even make any sense. Leslie had said something about Mustang already being taken, but Arthur couldn't make sense of that name either. The dumb thing on the guy's face made it even worse. Most people, including Quarter Horse called it a mustache, but Arthur had too much respect for mustaches to use that word. 'Thing' was more appropriate. Like someone had taken a patch of dog hair and glued it onto the idiot's lip.

"How in the hell is this guy worth thirty-grand? God help me."

Long orange extension cords stretched from the DJ's booth to the garage. Others went to light posts which were being erected to illuminate the yard when the party ran late. More desecrations, as far as the host was concerned. One of the purposes of ordering so many flowers was to cover the cords.

Quarter Horse leaned into the microphone. "Testing, testing!" His voice did not carry. He tried again. "Testing. Listen to my sexy voice…" Same result. "What the hell is going on here?"

Arthur couldn't take much more. There was still thirty-six more hours to endure. The party was at noon, and knowing this crowd, they would party well into the night. Cups and food would be everywhere, people puking after getting drunk…

He officially hated weddings. Before, he simply didn't care for them, but now he outright hated their existence. Every union should be in the courthouse from now on as far as he was concerned.

Idiot-stache over there only made it worse. His voice was grating, and the mic wasn't even working yet.

He stepped away from the booth and went to the garage. "Hey, Gordy! Is the cord plugged in?"

Someone with a voice as obnoxious as his name responded. "Hang on! Something's gone wrong in here. Nothing's working."

At that moment, the butler stepped out. "Pardon me for disturbing you sir, but we seem to be facing a bit of a problem."

"What is it?"

The butler gestured to the door. Arthur followed him into a dark house.

"The power's out."

"Oh, lovely," Arthur said.

The DJ and his assistant were already exclaiming the news to his wife and daughter.

"Problems with electricity! We have none!" Quarter Horse shouted.

Leslie's freakout was instantaneous. "No power?! Like, none at all?"

"Not unless you count the charge in my cell."

"Not funny!"

"What happened?!" Wanda said.

"Something with this electric box thing," Quarter Horse said.

Arthur made his way to the garage, finding Wanda and Leslie in hysterics.

"Oh, my God!" the bride-to-be cried out. She turned and buried her face in her fiancé's chest. "We won't be able to turn on the lights and play music. Our wedding is ruined!"

"Oh, for the love of God," Arthur muttered.

Wanda thrust a finger in his direction. "Knock it off. It's her…"

"Her big day. Yes, I get it." Arthur dug out his own smart phone and used it as a flashlight. "Son of a bitch. There's a bunch of shit shorted out. I don't even know where to begin."

"You knew this wedding was coming up and you never bothered checking for problems?!" Leslie said.

Arthur looked to Dale. *So glad she's to be yours.*

"Honey, I wasn't *aware* of this."

"Doesn't matter," Leslie said. "My special day is ruined. We may as well have just gone to the courthouse. Be worth just as much as this disaster."

Arthur shrugged. "Damn, had I known this would save me eighty-grand, I would've taken a blow torch to this thing…"

"Arthur!" Wanda's eyes turned fiery. Her husband shut his jaw and walked past her into the light.

"Relax, dear." He began scrolling through local contractors on the internet. "Let me find someone who can fix it…" He settled on a name. "Ah-ha! This guy sounds good."

CHAPTER 4

"God, that looks ugly."

Valentine Krane chuckled at his neighbor's expression as he looked at the thirty-foot gash that was in his lawn. It was as though his property was about to split in two. Dirt mounds lined the laceration, which traveled all the way to the main road.

"You asked for this," he said. Charles Netty pinched his lip between his teeth. Val recognized the look of someone who was having buyer's remorse. "I'll have it looking nice and pretty for you by the time you get back."

"Please do." He sighed. "I guess I picked a good time to visit my sister."

"By the time you get back Saturday night, I'll have it looking extra pretty."

"Better. So far, it looks like my lawn's been massacred."

Val smiled and nodded, keeping his wit in check. He wasn't sure what the guy expected when he arranged for underground cables to be installed on his property. It was an area teeming with trees, and on three separate occasions, storms had dropped branches on the cables. Lucky for Charles, he had an electrician living next door. Even with that convenience, it still grew tiresome worrying about the issue. Every time the wind picked up, Charles crossed his fingers in hopes the cables would remain intact.

Last time was the final straw.

Everything was cleared with the county. All that needed to be done was the installation itself.

Charles tossed his suitcase into his passenger seat. "I guess going to my sister's place beats having no a/c for a couple days. Barely."

"Yeah? She a talker?"

"Yes. About everything I hate talking about." Charles begrudgingly sank into the driver's seat. He closed the door behind him, continuing the conversation through the open window. "Politics, her last fight with Mom, politics, her gripes about work, politics, her second-to-last fight with Mom, politics, more gripes about work…"

"Politics?" Val added.

Charles smirked. "Did I forget to mention that one?" They both laughed.

"At least you got a new nephew out of the deal."

Charles was unfazed by thoughts of bundled joy. He shook his head slightly and pursed his lips.

"I guess. With that dumbass father of his, I don't know. The kid's cute now, but for all I know, I'm probably looking at a future delinquent. I swear that dumbass guy Sherrie's with *enjoys* getting arrested."

"Does he now?" It was all Val could think of to fill the awkward void when it was his turn to talk. "He, uh, a loser or something?"

"He's an ex-con. What do you think?"

Val pursed his lips. Charles had moved here three years ago, *after* the word about Val's background got out.

"I think he needs direction." Again, it was all he could think to say. This conversation had taken an awkward turn for him, though Charles was unaware. No way was he going to bring up his own past as an example. That would open the floodgates to inquisition about his background. 'What? You were in prison? How long? Six years? For what? Armed robbery and assault?'

That imaginary conversation did not seem so dramatic to Val, for it was based on real encounters. Many times over, he had to clarify aspects of the crimes, like the fact he did not really have a weapon. Then, when he did, it unintentionally came off as justifying his actions. 'I didn't actually have a gun, therefor robbing the place wasn't *that* big a deal.'

"More like a good kick in the ass," Charles said. "Who knows? Maybe I'm less forgiving than you."

Val shrugged. *No. It's just that I'm not one to talk.*

"Okay," Charles said, his tone that of someone who was growing bored with this conversation. He started the car and buckled in, then looked at the dirt line in his yard. "This *will* be done by the time I get back, right?"

"I promise," Val said, chuckling. "Believe me, when you get back, the trench won't even be on your mind."

"Sounds good to me. See you Sunday." Charles rolled up the window, and was quickly out of the driveway.

Val turned his attention to the lawn and the set of high-voltage cables he would spend the next twenty-four hours installing. For him, it wasn't just business, it was direction. The very direction he needed in his early twenties. Instead of direction and drive, he had debt, and a poor social circle who believed in selling illegal substances to make a living. Not having steady work led to bills piling up, his car being repossessed, and his landlord threatening to evict him. His attempts to land jobs fell short. As it turned out, they did not want to hire a loser who dressed in ragged clothing, with tattoos covering both arms, and an entitled attitude. Who knew?

Reflection on those days always made Val look at a reflection of himself. Today, his hair was short, his shirt tucked into the waist of blue jeans. If his clothes ever got dirty, it was only due to work, and not a crummy lifestyle. It was the lifestyle he adopted from his uncle. Uncle Bob was the one who taught him his craft, including the business aspect of it. He was the only one who had faith in Val, when everyone else, including Mom and Dad, had written him off as a failure.

Val even wore the watch Bob had left him. It was a simple twenty-dollar watch, nothing amazing, except that it was Bob's, and it made Val think of him every time he looked at it. The day he passed, Val made his vow to live straight from now on, no matter how tough things got financially.

Not that he felt any temptation to break the law to begin with. Six years in prison, housed with the worst people imaginable, was more than enough. Not to mention the battle to fix his reputation was hard fought. He felt grateful enough that the town, for the most part, had accepted him. Some of the deputies did not hide their caution when around him. He chalked it up to being in a low-crime area and them craving having something to do beyond checking fishing licenses.

"Okey-dokey. Time to work." He knelt by the cables and his tool kits, and recited something his uncle always said. "The greatest reward for work is not ease, rest, or immunity from work, but increased capacity, greater difficulty, and *more* work."

As though in response to that statement, his phone rang. Val stood up and put the device to his ear.

"Good morning. This is Valentine Krane speaking."

"Good morning Mr. Krane. My name's Arthur. I'm having an electrical issue in my garage. I think I have a box or something that needs to be replaced, and right away if possible. I'm in the big house on the north corner of Lake Lucas."

"Oh, good. I'm not far from there, actually. Let me pack some supplies, and I'll head right over."

"Excellent. I'll wait for you."

"Yes sir. See you soon." Val hung up, juggled his phone victoriously for a moment before clipping it to his belt. "Uncle Bob forgot to also mention *money.* Money, money, money, money!"

CHAPTER 5

"Oh, no. MOM!"

Wanda raced down the hill, bumping against a few of the set-up crew. Her wide girth compared to their slender frames was like a bowling ball plowing through some pins. She found Leslie, red-faced, standing by the union table. The bride-to-be had a cell phone in one hand and a crushed daisy in the other.

"What's the matter, dear?"

"It's the caterer!"

"What about him?"

"We ordered chicken as the main course, but he now claims he doesn't have enough for us. He thinks offering beef strips and steak is going to make up for his inability to plan!" Leslie slapped her forehead. "Is there anything else that can go wrong?"

One of the bridesmaids, Robin Berry stepped up. "Don't worry, sweetie!" She wrapped her arms around the teary-eyed Leslie. "Beef is my favorite. Add some noodles and broth to it, and yuuuuum-yum!"

"It's not what we ordered."

"It's a buffet! It's not like there won't be plenty of other food to eat," Robin said. She looked to Wanda and nodded slightly. *I got this.*

Wanda smiled, and headed back up the hill. The electrical contractor would be here any minute, and Wanda would rather she deal with him instead of Arthur. Knowing him, he would probably get the cheapest service available. Besides, Robin had been a friend of Leslie's for many years. They had known each other through high school, been to college together, and been on a few trips abroad. In a sense, Robin probably knew Leslie better than they did.

"What's the matter?"

When Wanda heard the question, she thought it was Arthur speaking. Instead, it was the nosey William Cook. A cantankerous individual, he was always sniffing like a dog.

Wanda suspected substance use, especially when she looked into his glassy eyes. She was no expert in the effects of narcotics, but it did appear like his pupils were dilated. Then there was the issue of his attitude. As expressed in his question, he was always putting himself in the middle of everything, as though he owned the place.

"Nothing," Wanda said. She pressed up the hill.

"It's something. Robin's having a little meeting with Leslie, by the looks of it."

Wanda stopped, then looked back.

"Robin's a bridesmaid. Leslie's the bride. They're friends. Do the math." She continued on. "Fucking prick." Why Robin was with that miserable bastard was beyond Wanda. Wanda knew she lived a spoiled lifestyle, and she didn't mind it one bit, but she and her daughter at least had decent tastes in men. Arthur was grumpy and cheap, but at the end of the day, he wanted the best for his family. Same with Dale Woods, Leslie's husband-to-be.

As Wanda approached the garage, she gave a glance in the direction of her daughter. She was still whining to Robin about the caterer. That didn't concern her. Leslie had proven herself to be something of a bridezilla, after all.

It was that jerk William Cook that brought her pause. The guy was heading over to Robin, on a mission to butt in.

Arthur stepped onto the front patio, immediately seeing his daughter up in arms. He groaned. "What's the matter now?"

"Just caterer stuff. You know Leslie. She wanted everything to be pitch-perfect, just the way she imagined it. Down to every blade of grass, the position of every cloud in the sky, the music, the moon... if anything's out of sync, she goes nuts."

"I told you we should've had her evaluated when she was six."

"She's *not* on the spectrum! You bring that up one more time!"

Arthur leaned against the wood rail. "Ooookay." He sipped on his glass, watching the setup resume.

"How many of those have you had?" Wanda said.

"Not enough."

"What has gotten into you? This is your only daughter's wedding!"

"I'm catering this? I'm buying hotels for every idiot in the wedding party. Is that not enough?"

Wanda stood, hands on her hips, shaking her head. "A moment ago, I was thinking of what a decent guy you are, only to find you standing up here with a drink in your hand at ten o'clock, like some lowlife drunk."

"Beg your pardon, but I'm catering this whole party." Arthur downed the glass. "Pardon me for relaxing at my *vacation home.*"

Wanda threw her arms up, fed up with this exchange. Relief came with the sound of tires on the driveway pavement. Immediately, one of the DJ crew stepped out of the garage and waved to them.

"The electrician guy is here."

"Thank God," Wanda said. She looked at Arthur. "You coming?"

"You have my checkbook," he said.

"Whatever."

"'Whatever.'" He redirected his attention to the gathering at the bottom of the hill. "What's *he* up do?"

Wanda saw who he was looking at, replied, "Who knows?" then disappeared into the garage. If there was anything she and her husband could agree on, it was that William Cook was a prick.

Leslie and Robin had moved their conversation to the dock. The bride had calmed down a bit, though she was giving Robin an earful of the stresses of managing this wedding.

"I just need this day to be perfect. I don't understand why everything is going wrong at the last minute. First, there's the issue with the flowers, then the electricity, now the caterer. It's like the whole world is out to get me." Robin put a hand on her shoulder, briefly looking away to roll her eyes without being noticed.

"Yeah, it really is a drag." *Even though your dad's paying for everything and your mom is doing the actual management. You were in charge of picking out your dress, making one or two phone calls, and... Yeah, that's about it.* Robin knew she needed to take Leslie's mind off the wedding. "Hey! You remember that trip we took to France?"

"Of course. I miss traveling."

"Me too. Haven't traveled in…" She could see William Cook in her peripheral vision. *Since him.* "Almost ten years, I think. God, I'm getting old. I wasted my precious twenties away, that's for damn sure."

She kept her eye on her boyfriend. He seemed to have stopped his approach, and was now pretending to admire the lake. Since a couple of months ago when he caught her venting about their relationship to one of her other friends, he assumed *every* private discussion was about him. Never mind the fact that this was a wedding and Leslie was visibly upset over every waking aspect.

In addition, it wasn't like Leslie would want to listen to Robin's complaints anyway. There was no denying this was a one-sided friendship. Every trip they went on, they did what Leslie wanted to do. Every college assignment they worked on, it was Robin doing ninety-percent of the work. If Leslie had a problem, Robin and whoever else around was expected to listen. The opposite never occurred, as evidenced by one dinner when Robin opened up to Leslie about some relationship difficulties. She was in the middle of describing a bad argument between her and William, only to realize Leslie was goofing around on her phone the entire time. To test whether her 'friend' was listening, she abruptly stopped talking and let the table go dead silent. There was no acknowledgement for about two minutes, after which Leslie realized the story was 'over' and said, "Oh, man. That sucks."

Robin hated being the good girl. Maybe it was a way of making up for negative aspects in her life. Things she kept close to the chest. Maybe it was her misery, or her desire to leave William. It wasn't clear if he knew her intentions. Unfortunately, she was low on funds and had nowhere to go.

She gazed at the lake. "It's beautiful here. No wonder you picked this place to have your wedding."

"Been coming here since I was little," Leslie said. "I just hope the weather holds up. I've always wanted an outside wedding, but now I'm afraid that'll be ruined too."

"No, I don't think the weather's out to get you too," Robin said.

"I hope so." Leslie brushed her hair back, making sure not a single strand was out of place. "Saturday's gonna be the perfect day. Just as I always imagined. Absolutely *nothing* will go wrong, that's why all the problems are happening now instead of Saturday."

Robin suppressed a laugh. Leslie was playing the part of the rich, spoiled bridezilla so well, it almost seemed like an act. There was not one ounce of self-awareness. God help her hubby-to-be for going through with this.

Leslie finally smiled. "Dale's opening another store. His brand is quickly growing into a franchise."

Robin nodded. Leslie boasting about her fiancé's financial success was a common point of conversation. It was difficult to ascertain if Leslie was deliberately rubbing it in, or was heedlessly leading into a monologue about the glorious years of traveling, parties, and vacation properties like her father's. It was likely the latter, though it sometimes felt as though she was rubbing it in. Leslie knew of Robin's financial problems. She was living paycheck-to-paycheck, with little to spend on luxuries.

Robin tolerated it, for it clearly elevated Leslie's mood. She watched the lake and the golden sunshine which reflected off its surface. It was good to appreciate the smaller things in moments like these. It helped suppress any feelings of jealousy or annoyance.

"Yeah, you've told me."

"Might be opening another one in a few months. It'll bring in five-hundred grand a year in profits."

"Damn!" Robin chuckled. "With that kind of money, along with what he's already bringing in, you could afford a small house for, say, a best friend?" She nudged her.

Leslie barely seemed to notice. "We're talking about getting me a Porsche, and maybe getting that vacation home in Florida we've been eyeballing."

Robin kept quiet, maintaining that smile. *Of course you are.*

"Oh! And we might take a trip to Australia soon. He's got a few connections there."

"Wow. Great."

"And we've got a house-cleaning service signed on. Thank God. I hate scrubbing dishes and doing laundry."

Robin stood up, unable to take it anymore. "I, uh, am gonna run to the house for a cup of coffee. You want one?"

"Yeah, sure. Two Sweet'n Lows."

"Sure thing." Robin marched from the dock, breathing a sigh of relief once she was several yards away. "Good lord, you spoiled bitch."

"Hey!"

Robin stopped and shut her eyes. All of a sudden, she wished she remained with the spoiled bride.

"Yes, William?"

He walked up beside her, scratching his chin as though somehow that would make him appear like he was innocently inquiring for casual conversation.

"Hey, babe. What were you talking about over there?"

She shrugged. "Just wedding stuff. Surprised?"

"Just, you know. You two seemed to make a point to head off on your own. There's a whole group of bridesmaids…"

"It's not like we have a conference every time a pair of us feels like chatting," Robin said.

He sniffed, though not to smell. Robin groaned, much to his annoyance. Only the presence of the setup crew and the rich Arthur Bowen prevented him from acting on his emotion. Barely.

"Something wrong?" He shifted back and forth, attempting to smile.

"Just getting coffee."

"What were you two talking about?"

"You already asked, and I already answered. Wedding stuff. By the way, you have your tux, right?"

"Of course I do! Why? You think I'd drop the ball?"

"No. You just waited till the last second, was all."

The shifting intensified. "You think I'm a screwup? That what you were talking about over there?"

"Oh, for Pete sake." Robin continued up the hill. William followed. Robin waved him off, grinning to a couple people she passed by in order to maintain the illusion that nothing was wrong. "William…" she spoke in a low hiss, "go the fuck away, please."

It wasn't her tone that made him stop, but the glare from Arthur Bowen. William was not the brightest, but he knew Arthur had funds and would easily bury him should he do anything to screw up this expensive celebration. William held back and lit a cigarette, watching Robin head in through the garage entrance.

Val shone his light over the junction box and the various piping which led to the outlets and lights. "Yep, the circuit breaker needs to be replaced. Might need a new subpanel too. Some wiring needs to be replaced here and there." He pointed at a couple areas.

Wanda nodded, not really understanding what he was explaining. There were only two aspects she gave a damn about.

"Let's get to the nitty gritty. Can it be done today, and how much will it cost?"

"Well, you're in luck. I happen to have the box and correct wiring on hand. This system is pretty similar to other properties around this lake, so it's pretty easy for me to figure it out. As for cost..." He pulled out his calculator and began jotting down notes.

"Here." Wanda pulled out the checkbook, wrote a number, and handed it to him. "Keep the change."

Val looked at the check. "Whoa! You sure?"

"Yes. I just want it done as soon as possible."

Val knew the tone. This family had money and was willing to spend it. At least, the wife was. As long as the check cleared, Val did not care.

"I'll get right on it."

Wanda smiled. "Thank you."

Val hurried out to his truck, grabbed his gear, then hurried back.

"What the...?! What are *you* doing here?"

Val stopped at the entrance, seeing the twenty-seven year old brunette staring at him. It took a second for his brain to catch up with his eyes. No doubt, it was the same Robin Berry from back in the day. Worse days.

For several moments, they stood in stunned silence, their eyes locked on the other.

"Robin?"

"Val? What are you doing here?"

"I was called to do some electrical work. What are *you* doing here?"

Robin kept her stern, inquisitive stare. "I'm part of the wedding party. When did you get out of prison?"

Wanda suddenly emerged. "Prison? What's this I hear about prison?" She looked at Val. "You a convicted felon, sir? You come here, scoping the place out?"

"What? NO! *You* called me. I run a business."

"Running a scam, are ya?" she continued. "We're not going to be cheated by some thief, Mr. Krane."

Val couldn't believe it. The lack of sense in her statement was past the point of comical. This Mrs. Bowen lady was suddenly nothing like the sensible woman he was speaking to three minutes ago.

In less than thirty seconds, this situation had gone from friendly to almost completely out of hand. Val needed to think quickly whether he wanted to continue this deal. The check was still in his possession. All he had to do was hand it back. As much as he hated the thought of losing business, any business, it was clear he was dealing with some highly spoiled individuals.

There's clearly no convincing these people of the matter.

Val went to hand the check back. "Maybe it's best you call another contractor." His glare shifted toward Robin. "Thanks a lot."

Wanda turned toward her. "You know this Valentine Krane?"

Val stood, check still in hand, the dumb woman more interested in digging into his past than letting him simply hand it back and leave. He didn't want to leave without making sure it was in her hand. People as crazy as she was appearing to be, for all he knew, would falsely accuse him of stealing it just for the power thrill.

"Well…" Robin's face showed a hint of regret. "It was a long time ago."

"What was he in prison for? Fraud? Theft? Breaking and entering?"

"Armed robbery and aggravated assault!"

Val gulped at the sight of William Cook. Six-foot-two and pale as ever, he was as angry to see Val as the last day they saw each other.

Oh, sweet baby Jesus, why is this happening?

32

Val thrust the check toward Wanda. "Listen, ma'am. Just take your ch—"

"This guy tried to kill me! Tried beating me and Robin up for no reason! *After* robbing a bank at gunpoint!"

Val's temper broke. "Listen, you filthy prick! You know that's a gross exaggeration. We got into it because..." His foot snagged on the DJ extension cable, causing him to stumble. Fighting to keep his balance, he collided against Robin with his shoulder, knocking her backward.

"At it again, huh, motherfucker?!"

"Wait, no..."

William threw himself onto Val. The situation exploded into a frenzy of fists and insults.

Val attempted to preserve some sense of reason by pushing him away instead of punching back. As a consequence, he absorbed a number of blows to the ribs and shoulder.

"Get off! GET OFF!"

There was no reasoning with this madman. The situation had exploded from zero to a million, and more people were piling in. One of those swings caught Val on the chin. Finally, the beast was unleashed.

Val struck back, clocking William in the nose.

"Val stop!" Robin cried.

"What's happening!" cried a hysterical Leslie from the bottom of the hill.

Wanda was on the phone. "Yes, I need the police here right away."

****

"... and if you understand the pressures building up directly under the Yellowstone caldera, you'd realize that the United States has less than seventy years before an eruption.

"You say that, but there's a lot of evidence that suggests otherwise. If we were that close, there'd be greater elevation in the landmass. That pressure you spoke of could force the ground upward over a period of time..."

"Switch that crap off, would ya?" Taylor said.

"Hell no," Alan said. "It's interesting. I'm learning about super volcanos. How can you not find that interesting?"

"It would be interesting if these people were real scientists, not a couple twenty-year old know-it-alls with nothing more to their credibility than a microphone, and dumbasses willing to give them an audience."

Alan switched off the podcast. "Well, fine then. I guess you'll just have to listen to me talk." Taylor groaned. She wasn't sure which was worse. Her reaction sparked laughter from her fellow deputy.

The dispatcher's voice filled the vehicle. *"Any available unit, we have an assault in progress at the Bowen property, located at the north end of the lake."*

Taylor shut her eyes and threw her head back. "Just my luck. This day in which I have a migraine the size of... Yellowstone... a call like this comes in."

"Hey, you've spent all morning bitching about boredom," Alan said. He pulled the mic to his lips. "Car Three copies. We're on our way."

"Copy that, Three."

Taylor found a place to turn around. "I'm gonna kill you."

"I'll buy you some Tylenol." He switched on the lights, then whooped as Taylor floored the accelerator.

****

The melee continued, attracting the attention of far off boaters. People fishing on the lake and walking the various trails gathered at the shorelines to watch the chaos from afar.

Leslie Bowen was as furious as her parents. Her shouts were lost in the jumble of chaotic shouting which filled the air. William and Val were going at it, the latter doing his best to fend Robin's crazed boyfriend off.

Arthur Bowen, now more aggravated than ever, threw himself into the mix.

"What the hell?! Get out of here!"

Wanda raised her phone as though it were a winning lottery ticket. "I called the police! They'll be here any minute!"

Several setup crew converged on the brawlers, finally getting between them and forcing them apart.

"I'm good," Val said, holding his hands up. He was appreciative of their efforts, for it was nearly impossible to keep the psycho off.

"You don't seem 'good'," one of the guys said. Val could feel their grips tightening.

"Let go. I'm not gonna…"

"We'll just hang on to you until the cops get here."

Meanwhile, the fellas who pulled William away had promptly let him go. They stood in front of him to make sure he wouldn't resume the brawl, but other than that, they had assumed he was the victim in this case. It came as no surprise to Val when William started playing the part as such.

"You saw that, right! He came at Robin and Mrs. Bowen!" He turned to the crowed like a celebrity caught in a scandal. "You know what happened, right?!"

"Will, stop it!" Robin said.

"You saw what he did!"

Flashing lights and echoing sirens drew everyone's attention. The police SUV parked on the side of the driveway. Two officers stepped out. Taylor Davies and Alan Goldstein. Good and bad news for Valentine Krane. Over the course of the last couple of years, he had interacted with both. Taylor was mild-mannered and treated him like a normal individual, while Alan always acted as though Val was carrying contraband in his pocket. As soon as the guy saw him, there was a noticeable spring in his step.

Alan leaned over to Taylor, not bothering with discretion. "See? I told you he was trouble."

"Shh."

"Still in denial." Alan approached the crowd. "Good morning everyone. What's going on?"

Several fingers pointed at Val, and a few at William. Alan ignored the latter, focusing on the one who was still being restrained by the staff.

"Six years in prison wasn't enough for you, Mr. Krane?"

"No, Alan," Val said. "This is a misunderstanding that got way out of hand."

"Seems that's the common excuse. Just a misunderstanding," Alan said.

"Damn right!" William said. "He assaulted my girlfriend here, just like he did several years ago when he attacked us. He's a violent criminal. A bank robber. Attempted murderer!" He sniffed, rubbed his nose. "Arrest him!"

Taylor stepped forward. "You alright sir?"

William tilted his head back. "He struck me in the chin and once on the cheek."

"No. You're acting as though you're having trouble breathing." She leaned forward to get a look at his eyes.

William quickly backed off. "Why are you questioning *me*?! He's the criminal!"

"Mr. Cook, shut the hell up," Arthur said.

"I understand you're putting together a wedding celebration," Taylor said. "What's Mr. Krane's involvement?"

"I called him because I thought he was an electrician."

"I *am* an electrician," Val said.

"I heard Wanda claim you were a scam artist, and you seemed in a hurry to leave after that," he said.

"No. I could sense that this situation was going downhill fast and I wanted to leave, but not before handing back the check first."

"He got highly agitated when his criminal past got brought up," Wanda said.

Alan turned toward his suspect. "Well, well, well, Mr. Krane. So much for rehabilitation, huh?"

"Alan…" Taylor took him by the shoulder and leaned into his ear. "Shut up."

"What's with your obsession with this guy? You have a crush?"

"What's with your obsession with treating him like he's Hitler?" she replied, then turned to face Robin. "Is it true? He assaulted you?"

"No! It's not true. He tripped over this stupid cord right here." Robin kicked the orange extension cable stretched over the concrete.

"They used to be in a relationship," William said. "I suspect it was abusive, considering how she's always so timid around him. Even now, with you here, she's afraid to say the wrong thing."

Val scoffed. "The lack of self-awareness with this asshole is astounding."

"Is this true?" Wanda said.

"Can we get this resolved, please?!" Leslie shouted.

"Ma'am!" The DJ approached the deputies, phone in hand. "For what it's worth, I caught the whole thing on video."

"Okay, good. I appreciate your help in the matter."

"Well, I thought it'd be a cool story to share on my social media site," the DJ said.

Taylor moaned. For one split-second, it seemed there was at least one person in this crowd that wasn't batshit insane. At least there was video evidence of the recording, which would settle the matter.

Alan stood beside her, arms crossed, ready to watch Valentine Krane take a wild swing at the crowd.

Right there on the screen was the suspect, paper check in hand, being extended toward Wanda Bowen.

"Listen, ma'am. Just take your ch—"

The screen whipped toward a lively William Cook. *"This guy tried to kill me! Tried beating me and Robin up for no reason! After robbing a bank at gunpoint!"*

Back to William.

"Listen, you filthy prick! You know that's a gross exaggeration. We got into it because…"

It was clear as day. He tripped on the cord and fell against Robin. Ten seconds later, William was all over him.

Taylor dug out a card from her wallet and handed it to the DJ. "You mind emailing that video to the address listed here?"

"I guess so."

"I appreciate it." Taylor looked to Alan. "Looks like a misunderstanding."

"What?" William threw his hands in the air. "What are you talking about?"

"I said, it was a misunderstanding," Taylor said, more sternly this time. William backed off, but only thanks to the look he was getting from Arthur.

The rich lawyer approached Robin. "Why'd you call him out if he wasn't threatening you?"

"I… I…" Robin stammered, unable to get a sentence out.

"Told you she's intimidated by him," William said.

"No, I…"

Taylor raised her hands. "Guys, let's dial it down."

Alan sneered. "You saw at the beginning of the video. He has it out for this guy here." He tilted his head toward William. "Isn't that the fella he was arrested for assaulting?"

Taylor so badly wanted to tell him off, but knew he had a point in this instance. Alan must have read that police report a hundred times over. Right now, all she wanted was for this call to be over and done with. It was a situation where only the video told the truth, and only a partial truth at that. The video started five seconds before Val tripped. Everything that led up to it was speculation. She couldn't deny Val was agitated in the footage, though she suspected it was because everyone was ganging up on him.

Either way, it was a bad coincidence that this situation involved the same people he victimized in the past.

Taylor walked up to Val. "I need you to leave the property."

"I was going to. But they wouldn't…"

"Val… stop talking. Just get in your truck and leave. Please."

Val stared her in the eye. He was a man forever scorned by his history, so much so, that even the people in his corner had to treat him as suspect, even when the evidence was in his favor.

Without saying a word, he got in his truck and left. He kept a close eye on the other vehicles. With everyone eager to villainize him, he didn't want his vehicle to draw too close to the others parked in the driveway. For all he knew, someone might claim he was driving aggressively and nicked their vehicle.

Only when he was back on the road did he finally apply pressure to the accelerator. His mind was racing, attempting to absorb what had just happened. Right then, he had a realization.

"Shit!" He had left the supplies in the driveway, having dropped them during the brawl. Several hundred dollars' worth of supplies, lost stupidly thanks to that jerk William Cook.

Of all people to visit this town, it *had* to be Robin and William.

He had no choice but to write it off as a loss. Going back was suicidal, and making any kind of request could easily be twisted into a narrative that he's harassing those 'poor lawyers'.

Val pressed on. Right now, all he could do was go about his day and try and forget this ever occurred.

****

After watching Val leave the property, Taylor turned to the group. "Alright. Excitement's over. Please, everyone try and have a good wedding."

"I don't know how that's possible!" Leslie said.

"Oh, God," Arthur muttered. "Thank you, Officers. Sorry for all the trouble."

"Yep." Taylor walked away, shaking her head. *Right, lawyer man. Like you didn't add to it yourself by baiting Val into incriminating himself with your questioning.*

She got in the SUV and grabbed the mic. "Car Three to dispatch. Everything's alright over here at the Bowen property. I'll be heading in to fill out a small report. We're chalking it up to a misunderstanding, provided with video evidence."

"Copy that, Three."

Alan took the passenger seat. "Well, that was fun."

"You sound disappointed. Were you hoping to use those cuffs?"

"I'm not that much of a jerk. You should know me better than that, Davies."

"That's exactly it. I *do* know you. You're a little too eager to rush headfirst into trouble."

Alan put his foot up on the dashboard and leaned back. "We're cops. Isn't that what we're paid to do?"

Taylor started the engine. What was there to say? Alan was set in his attitude, and nothing she could say would change that. At least this altercation gave her an excuse to head to the station, where they kept Tylenol in the lounge cabinets.

Two of those capsules would partially quell the issue. What she really needed was for three o'clock to get here so she could go home and bury her face in a pillow. Bedtime would come early today.

****

"The hell you all standing around for?!" Wanda said to the crowd. "I'm not paying you to spectate. Back to work."

39

The crowd dispersed. The setup crew resumed their duties, all the while talking amongst themselves about the craziness that recently occurred. The DJs returned to their equipment, only to realize they still couldn't test it because no electrical work had been done to the house.

A furious Arthur Bowen joined his wife by the driveway. A lit cigar was crunched between his teeth. Wanda demonstrated her revulsion of tobacco with a loathing grimace.

Arthur crossed his arms. "Oh?! There a problem?"

"You really want to start with me?"

"Excuse me?!" He removed the cigar from his mouth, pointing it at her as though it were a sixth finger. "You decide to get all psycho-emotional about the contractor dude, and start a brawl in my yard."

"Your yard?"

"Yes, *my* yard!"

"Will you two stop!" Leslie cried out. "You're ruining my wedding!" Finally, her fiancé emerged from the crowd and took her by the shoulders.

"It's okay, babe."

"It's not okay, Dale."

"Oh, for chrissake." Arthur waved a hand dismissingly. "Your wedding will be fine. It's in two days." He planted the cigar between his teeth. "Not soon enough, I might add."

"Pardon me?" Wanda said, leaning in. "Say something there?"

He looked away. "No."

"You not care that your daughter enjoys her big day?"

"I'm more concerned about *him*," Arthur said, pointing at Dale. "Thanks to you, he's gonna have to deal with a spoiled brat for all his life."

Leslie stepped back, gasping with the same urgency as though she had been given a terminal diagnosis.

Wanda raised her hand back to smack him.

Robin rushed toward them, her boyfriend reaching out to grab her.

"Stop Robin!"

She ignored William and reached the arguing couple. "Please! This has already gotten out of hand. Let's not have another fight."

Wanda, Leslie, and Arthur looked to her, equally unpleased to see her, doubly so with the bastard standing behind her.

"Oh, you're worried about this getting out of hand?" Arthur said. "Wasn't it *you* who first called out that convict?"

Robin backed up. "What? No. I was just surprised to see…"

"And then your jackass boyfriend had to stick his nose into it, like he always does," Wanda said, pointing at William.

"We still don't have power," Leslie said. "And look!" She pointed at the family portrait that had fallen over. "I can't believe you, Robin! Look at this! It's broken. I was going to have it placed up in front at the ceremony. Now I can't, because you and dipshit couldn't contain your emotions."

William covered his mouth, failing to suppress his cackling. "Really? *We're* the ones who can't control our emotions. You, who can't stop from whimpering every two seconds, are judging others on…"

Robin elbowed him in the ribs.

"Some friend you are," Leslie said. It took a second for Robin to realize that statement was directed at her. She faced Leslie, who was marching into the house.

"Leslie, wait. This isn't my fault."

"I'm sick of things going wrong. Dad thinks the wedding party   is   too   big,   anyway." Robin stopped, reading between the lines. "You're kicking me out of the wedding?!"

Leslie didn't answer, slamming the door behind her. "IT'S DARK IN HERE!"

"I'm calling another electrician," Arthur said. He puffed on his cigar, scowling at Robin and William. "Looks like you two have caused enough trouble around here." He cocked his head in the direction of the vehicles. "Hope you enjoyed your stay."

"But."

"No buts," Wanda said.

Robin couldn't believe it. Her goal of reuniting Wanda, Arthur, and Leslie had been accomplished, though by an unexpected means. She had not intended to become their common enemy.

"Oh, come on," William said. "Are you guys serious?"

"Get out of here, druggie," Arthur said.

"What?! I don't…"

"Oh, please," Wanda said. "Are you two gonna vacate, or do I have to call the police back?"

Robin marched for the car. "I'm going! I'm going. Apparently, I'm no friend, anyway. Amazing how everyone was fine with me for over a decade, but whatever."

Midway through the driveway, she saw the equipment dropped by Val. The poor guy, flustered by the situation, had forgotten his stuff. No way was he going to return and collect it, knowing the craziness he would be walking into.

"Hmm."

A decision had to be made quickly. With that in mind, she collected the box and wiring, then took it to her vehicle. She opened the back seat and placed it beside her purse. She was glad she left it in the vehicle, for it would have made for an awkward situation had she left it in the house.

Her bags were still in the trunk. When they arrived, they had gone straight to work helping with the setup. It was another patch of good luck in this unlucky scenario.

Robin got in the driver's seat and turned the ignition.

William got into the passenger seat. "Good riddance. Don't know about you, but I'm ready to leave the house of dysfunction."

"Oh, you're one to talk."

"What does that mean?"

Robin shook her head, then steered out in the direction of town.

William bobbed his head like a bird, waiting for an answer. His hand tapped the armrest, annoying Robin all the more.

"I thought you were getting clean."

"I am."

She looked at his shaking hands. "I'm tired of this, William."

"That right? You liked it back in the day."

"Well, I was really stupid back in the day."

"You seem extra agitated with me."

"Oh my God." Robin nearly slammed her head against the steering wheel. "How could I not? With you, the way you are?"

"Oh, *I'm* the problem? Funny, you've been extra pissy since dickface showed up."

"You mean Valentine?"

"That's what I said. Dickface." He smiled. "It's a shame that DJ caught the thing on video. Personally, I would've found it hilarious if dickface got arrested and sent back to prison. Then dickface would have an all-too-literal meaning for another six years…"

Robin slammed on the brakes. Momentum drove William's head into the dashboard.

"Motherfucker!"

Robin put the car in park, got out, and strutted for the trunk. William watched her in the mirror, leaping out when he saw her pulling his duffle bag out.

"Hey! What the hell are you doing?!" Before he got close enough to yank it away, Robin tossed it into the ditch. "You crazy bitch! My stuff is in there!"

"Yep, I know." Robin shut the trunk and passenger door, then returned to her seat. "I was counting on it."

William turned around, seeing her inching away. "HEY!"

Robin poked her head through the window. "Call a cab. I'm done with you!" She floored the accelerator, speeding into the distance, leaving a furious William Cook screaming absurdities.

CHAPTER 6

As the excitement on the north end of the lake came to a close, the various spectators in their boats and walking the shore began to scatter. One boat, a standard aluminum twelve-footer, remained in place. Its two chubby occupants kept their eyes on the expensive-looking property on the hill. The drama they just witnessed was immeasurably entertaining, and they did not want to risk missing any possible follow-up.

Jerry Hart dug into the cooler. "As Will Ferrell said: Boy… that escalated quickly." He raised a beer and twisted the top off. Who cares if it was still morning. On these fishing trips, beer was as essential as water. Same with cigars and jerky.

His buddy, Max Lederman, was way ahead of the game. He was already halfway through his first bottle of Corona, a stogey, and a bag of Jack Links beef jerky. Jerry often joked that this was why Max was fifteen pounds heavier. Max didn't care. Being in his late forties, he had fully accepted that he was no Brad Pitt. Health food was a chore, both in consumption and prep. In his view, cooking anything that didn't come out of a can was a practically an art project.

Growing bored with watching the property, Max decided to resume fishing. He tossed his spinner bait sixty feet out, and slowly brought it back. No luck.

"Wouldn't it be hilarious if it rained on their precious ceremony?" he said.

"That's the risk you run with outdoor weddings," Jerry said. He took a swig of his beer. "Oh, wait. I forgot! Didn't you hear the lady? Saturday is going to be her perfect day. *Nothing* will go wrong!"

"Right?! Didn't you know? When you're rich enough, you can control the weather!" Their cackles echoed across the lake, drawing looks from the people on shore. Jerry watched the people conversing amongst themselves. "We better get a move on before we get sucked into the next drama spectacle."

44

Max reeled in his line and pulled up the anchor. "Where to?"

"You're the driver. You pick."

"I don't know. What sounds good? Middle of the lake? Some secluded cove?"

Jerry choked on his beer. "Jesus, dude. Way to make it sound like we're sneaking off for gay sex."

This time, it was Max who choked. "Thanks for that image." He spat a piece of jerky into the water.

"Lose your appetite, did ya?" Jerry tapped his stomach. "Was that a not-so-subtle remark at my shape? Ever take a look at yourself?"

"Riiight… because if you looked like Ryan Reynolds, it totally would make it all better…" Max shut his eyes in disgust. "Alright, can we end this really weird dumpster fire of a conversation and figure out where we're gonna go next? To *fish*?!"

Jerry pointed at the main body of the lake. "Let's just head that way until we find a suitable spot." He recoiled from the statement. "Shit. No matter how I put it, it still sounds like were looking a spot for a different kind of rod action…"

"Holy fuck, dude! Is there something else in that bottle other than beer?" Max started the outboard and steered the boat south. "I'm gonna have to rethink future fishing trips with you."

"Yeah? Well, I'm way ahead of you. Especially after the fumes I've had to deal with ever since you ate those breakfast burritos."

"Just means my exhaust system is healthy."

"Not sure you and healthy belong in the same sentence."

"Ha-ha-ha." Max pointed at Jerry's midsection. "Because you are totally one to talk. Fat ass."

"Fat-*ter* ass," Jerry said, pointing back at him.

"Wow, you're so clever." Max shoved a fresh piece of jerky between his teeth and dug into his vest for another cigar. Both men started cackling at their juvenile humor, smoking and drinking for nearly a mile down the lake.

Carelessly, they traveled down the neck of the lake. Soon, they reached a bend where it branched off into a series of coves while the main body arched west, then back to the south. Both men, now two beers into their day, got lost in a conversation about groundhogs in Jerry's yard before they realized they were on a collision course with a patch of cattails.

"...And the stupid traps won't work," Jerry said. "The furry little bastards just go right under the spikes, and on their merry way... Uh, dude? You intentionally running us aground?"

"Sorry." Max turned the prop, steering the boat to the right. "Kinda blacked out there."

"Might have to take it easy on them beers."

"More like take it easy on the number of bullshit groundhog stories I have to listen to. Doesn't take much to put somebody in a catatonic state."

Jerry lit a fresh cigar, ignoring his friend's insult. After slapping a mosquito that attempted to feed on his neck, he watched the trajectory of their boat. Up ahead to the left was a cove with several trees stretching over the water. Where there was shade, there was usually fish.

"Let's try this spot. Plenty of cover. Nobody else around.... Oh, shit... still sounds like..."

"Don't even say it!"

Jerry chuckled, having intentionally agitated Max.

Max slowed the boat and turned to port. All of a sudden, his eyes were wide, and a devious grin came over his face. "Well, well, well... looks like this was the perfect place after all for some sin..."

Jerry leaned away from him. "Dude! I was kidding!"

"Shh!" Max killed the motor and nodded at the end of the cove. "Shut up. You'll ruin the... ah, damn it! They see us."

Jerry looked, then whistled. "Oh! Well, lookie-lookie!"

As it turned out, they weren't alone after all. On the shore, partially obscured by the trees were two college age girls. There was no doubt of their activities, considering their horizontal position and the fact that they had stripped to their underwear.

The couple quickly learned the problem with secluded spots: everybody sought them out. They spotted the fishermen, then immediately started gathering their things.

"Aw. Don't feel you have to stop because of us!" Jerry said. One of the ladies raised a middle finger. Jerry put his arms out. "What? You tango out in the open, you run the risk of an audience, baby!"

"Screw yourself!" the other one shouted. They pulled on their shorts and tank tops, then disappeared into the woods.

Max sighed, longingly watching the trees. "Damn!"

"This day is suddenly no longer boring!" Jerry said. "Man. If only we arrived thirty seconds later. Would've gotten even more of a show."

"If you weren't so damn loud, we probably would have anyway," Max said. He tossed the empty bag of jerky at Jerry. "Had to ruin it with that high-pitched voice of yours."

Jerry picked up his rod and impaled a nightcrawler on the hooks. "You gonna sit there and bitch, or you gonna drop that anchor?"

Max let the five-pound weight in the water, letting the rope run along his fingers until it hit the bottom. He tugged gently, keeping the slack out, and tied it to the cleat on the stern. While tying the knot, he glanced at their surroundings.

"Lot of coves around here. Maybe they're moving on to the next one."

"Maybe. Maybe not," Jerry said. "Good chance their drive took a nosedive after seeing your saggy face."

"Doubt that, considering their view of me was mostly obstructed by *you*."

"Ha!" Jerry turned to look at him. "Max, there isn't much in the world that could obscure anyone's view of you."

Max looked at the sky, seeking strength from his maker. He wasn't sensitive about his weight, but the jokes were getting old fast today. Especially from Jerry. Adding to his frustration was the swaying of the boat.

"Hey! You forget you have an anchor on your end?"

Jerry placed his rod down and reached for the weight. He tossed it into the water and took out the slack until the line was taut. With no cleat on the bow, he had to tie the knot around a small metal loop at the tip. To do so, he had to lean over the water.

Just as he feared, Max bumped the boat, forcing him to catch himself. Jerry looked back. "Bastard."

"Serves you right."

Jerry pointed a finger. "You make me fall, you're a dead man." After cautiously watching Max for a few additional moments, he finally braved the task yet again. He leaned over, ass crack peeking over the waist of his pants. He brought the back half of the rope over the taut part, ready to fasten a knot to keep the anchor tight.

Using his mass, Max shifted the boat.

"Max you fu—"

Over he went. *SPLASH!*

Max leaned back and roared. Tears streamed down his face, his hands slapping his knees.

"OOOH! You dumb…" Suffocating laughter drowned out his sentence. Red faced and out of breath, Max looked at the rippling water. "I can't believe you fell for it." It took multiple deep breaths for him to regain control. Now, it was time to brave the wrath of his friend. Wherever he was.

Slowly, he moved into the bow section, cautiously watching the water. Jerry hadn't come up yet, immediately causing suspicion. Max was afraid to look over the side, thinking Jerry was lurking just under the gunwale, waiting to grab him and pull him down for some payback.

"Not happening, man. Come on up."

Another minute passed, and still there was no sign of Jerry. The water was still rippling, indicating some kind of movement was taking place under the water.

"Alright man, joke's over. I'll buy you a steak dinner, make it up to ya." Still no response. Now, Max was starting to feel concerned. Despite this, he was still suspicious that looking over the side was a trap. The water here was five feet deep at most. All Jerry had to do was stand up and he would be above water.

Max's mind began playing through the undesirable scenarios, however unlikely they were. If Jerry was drowning, it would not look favorably on Max, regardless of how it happened.

Finally, he leaned over the side, anticipating seeing a large figure reaching out and grabbing him.

"Alright, man. Nice try…" He froze, seeing a piece of fabric drifting over the rippling surface. A few inches away was another one. And another. Some were tan in color, others white. Khakis and t-shirt pieces! Like confetti from a birthday party, bits of shredded clothing drifting throughout the red water.

Red water…

It was a dark red cloud, gradually expanding.

"Jerry?!"

Up ahead, something drifted near the surface. It was fairly sizable, roughly the size of a man's forearm.

Max studied the item, spotting stringing substance extending from its stump, a white jagged thing protruding from its middle, and five digits on the other end.

It *was* a man's forearm.

Max stared blankly, watching the limb drift before sinking, as though tossed aside from something down below. It was the smell that finally made Max grasp the ugly reality that Jerry had just been torn apart.

"Oh, Jes—" Max's attempt to scream ended abruptly after his hand slipped, causing him to fall against the gunwale. Once again, he was staring straight into the water.

A large mass was right under the surface, two black eyes staring back at him. It's body was pancake shaped and rigid, black in color. Several legs protruded from each side, like a spider... or a *crab*.

Two arms burst from the surface. Scissor-like pincers sliced into Max's shoulders, and pulled him off the boat with minimal effort.

Once again, his scream was drowned out, this time by water. That didn't stop him from trying.

His abductor pinned him to the mucky lake bottom, where it proceeded to surgically make him lose weight. It started with both of his forearms, tossing them aside in favor of the meat in the torso area.

It pierced the midsection with its claws and cut upwards. The lake took the liquid contents like blood and urine, the crab took the intestines, muscle tissue, and organs. It enjoyed this meal in peace, not having to fight its brethren over it, for they were busy with the other one.

CHAPTER 7

"Anything else?"

Val tapped his fork against the plate, hardly looking up at the waitress. "Just coffee, please."

"As you wish." She went for the counter, her pacing that of someone eager to avoid an awkward conversation. As usual, word got around of the ex-con who got in a spat with his ex.

Val was feeling the lack of motivation that came with depression. Throughout the day, he managed to place the cable in his neighbor's yard. Even that required an extra kick in the ass to get done. It was hours before he overcame the jitters from the ruckus at the Bowen property.

Being overdue for a grocery trip, he only had a few options for dinner, none of which appealed to him. That, and he did not feel like cooking and making dishes. He came close to ordering pizza, only to decide he would rather get out of the house for a while.

The Pine Tree Café was a low-key place, much like the town in general. Half of the people who came here were regulars, the rest from out of town. The waitresses knew him by name, for he stopped in at least once every two weeks. Living alone, it felt nice to get out.

Today, he was regretting that decision. His food was mostly untouched. It was hard to eat when he could feel dozens of eyes boring into him. The awareness of attention heightened his senses. He could pick up faint whispers from across the room.

"That guy almost beat up a chick at that lawyer's property."

"I hear he pulled a gun at a bank once."

"I've heard he's nice. Maybe it's an act."

"Wonder what else he did. Criminals are only convicted for a fraction of the crimes they actually commit."

"The wait staff don't seem to like him."

The stereotypes of small towns was exemplified here in Bowling Pines. Gossip got around fast, and the more it got around, the more people began to speculate. Each rumor was instantly treated as fact, regardless of lack of evidence or foundation.

He heard the thud of a coffee mug touching down. Val looked up, thinking the waitress had returned with a fresh mug instead of replenishing his current one. His heart fluttered, and not due to caffeine intake.

"Hi, Val."

For the second time, Valentine Krane was unexpectedly face-to-face with Robin Berry. The decision to come to a café seemed worse than ever. He immediately eyed the exit. He could pay his tab at the front counter, and be out the door in sixty seconds.

Robin slipped into the opposite side of the booth. "You know, when someone says 'hi', it's usually polite to respond."

Val pressed his palms to the edge of the table, ready to push himself to his feet at a moment's notice.

"What are you doing here?" Realizing the pitch of his voice, he took a moment to cool his jets. "You track me down?" He glanced across the café, then out the window. "Where's your posse?"

Robin tapped her fingertips against the table, then smiled at the waitress as she arrived with Val's refill.

"Oh, hi. Can I get you something?"

Val's chest tightened. "No."

"Yes, actually!" A delighted Robin said. "I'll take a coffee, a roll, and a couple of eggs. Sunny side up, please and thank you."

The waitress jotted the order down. "You got it." She was gone in a flash, leaving a disgruntled Val staring across the table.

Robin smiled. Seeing that annoyed glare was nostalgic. "I remember getting such looks whenever I nagged you to run to the market and get me a latte. You'd say something like 'we have a coffee machine *here*!'" She chuckled. "I remember those days like they were yesterday."

Val's expression stayed firm. "You seem fond of those memories."

"Well, some of them."

"Yeah? Which ones? The one where I caught you shellacking that cocaine-addicted knucklehead." Val glanced around a second time. "Where is he, anyway? Last thing I need is to get in a brawl here of all places. It may not look like much, but I at least feel welcome here." All of a sudden, he could feel the stares coming from numerous other tables. "Most of the time, that is."

"No, no. At ease," Robin said, putting her hands ups. "None of them are here. This place is too... how should I put it... low-class for them." She gave it a meaningful glance. "I see why you like it, though. It's got that small town charm."

"That's why you're here?" he said. "Looking for small town charm?"

"Looking for *you*, actually."

"Great." Val tore at his eggs with his fork. It was the only damage he could do and get away with. "I know it's a small town, but how the hell did you manage to find me here? You become a detective in the past several years?"

"I'd make a good one," she said. She paused while the waitress brought her a cup of coffee. Cupping the warm mug in her hands, she leaned against the table. "To be honest, I drove all over the place, hoping I'd see your truck. Eventually, my search led me here. Well... my stomach led me here, but nonetheless, I pull in and here you are."

"Right... because phone numbers don't exist." Val crossed his arms. "You do realize you could've looked up my business online, right?"

"Yeah, sure. You mean to say you wouldn't have hung up the instant I identified myself?"

Val considered lying with a 'no, of course not' but instead went with a shrug. "Alright, maybe you have a point." He stalled by taking a prolonged swig of his coffee. During which, he eyed Robin's features. Her hair was a bit shorter than it used to be, and lacked the curls. She had been using a straightener. Her skin was tan as ever. She had gained a few pounds, though by no means was fat. It was actually an improvement over her skinny, younger self.

"You never answered my question."

"I just said, I drove around..."

"Where is *he*?"

"Oh. William." She shook her head. "I dumped him. Finally. And literally." Val straightened in his seat, his eyebrows slowly rising. There was no melancholy in Robin's voice. She acknowledged this change in relationship status with a restrained glee.

"'Literally'?"

"Yeah. I dumped his ass out of the car after leaving the Bowens."

"Wait? What the hell happened after I left?" Val asked. "Aren't you part of the wedding?"

"Was. Apparently, the drama I caused was too much for Leslie's sensibilities. They kicked us out."

"Wait, what?"

"Yep. Didn't bother to reimburse me for that stupid dress she made us get." Robin stuck out her tongue. "Actually, they did me a favor in a sense. That dress was not my taste."

"Too heavy?"

"Too slutty," Robin said. She was surprised to see Val chuckle. He stopped abruptly, as though having realized his irritable demeanor had shown vulnerable chinks.

"How so?" he said, looking away as to pretend not to be interested.

"Jesus, where do I begin?" she said. "First of all, there's no back. Second of all, the top comes up to like… here." She leveled her hand over her chest, resting it where her nipples were. "Also, the garment pushes the twins together as though we're cosplaying as some comic book bridal party fantasy."

Val stared into the distance, fully embracing that image. Robin leaned forward again, knowing full well what was going through his mind.

"You know, it's been a long time, but I still know you."

He returned to reality, his disquiet from her presence front and center. That glorious image of her in the wedding dress was swept away by flashes of William Cook, buck naked, bleeding into the carpet. To this day, Val could feel the tightening of handcuffs over his wrists, and that sunken feeling of being pushed into the back of a police car.

"Maybe not as well as you think," he said. "Why are you looking for me? Broke and looking for money again? Let me guess, you're about to lose your house again, and you need someone to pay the bills."

"No," she said. "I'm working. Still in the house. The monthly mortgage is being paid on time. Nice to have it remain in the family."

"Really? I would've figured you lost it after I got arrested."

"Well, the cops recovered most of the money. *Most* of it. Considering you took over a million bucks, it was easy enough for the cops to miss a few grand…or ten."

Val clenched his teeth. The urge to bring his fist down on the table was repressed only thanks to his uncle's teachings. Still, knowing he essentially paid room and board for William Cook brought him on the edge of violating his oath.

"Lovely. While I was rotting in prison, you were shacking up with Snow White."

Robin's expression soured. "You have every right to be angry."

"That's putting it mildly."

They both sat quietly, faces tense, while the waitress brought Robin's food order. Immediately, she could sense the friction between them.

"Everything alright here?" she asked.

"Oh yes," Robin said, forcing a smile. "Perfectly fine. Thank   you."
The waitress nodded, then waited a couple additional moments, waiting for any hidden gesture from the young lady signaling for help. When she received none, she continued about her business.

Robin picked at her food, her appetite having waned in the past couple of minutes.

"That brings me back to why I came looking for you," she said. "I, uh, wanted to say thanks for what you did."

Val leaned back, waving his hand dismissively. "Robin, thanking me for providing money for you to shack up with Cook… it's a little insulting."

"No, not that. For not… telling the court about me."

Val relaxed his posture. For a moment, he was back in the police station, then at the courthouse months later. Both times, they tried to get him to give up the accomplice that was with him during the robbery. After all, someone was driving the getaway car. They even offered him a plea deal should he give up the driver.

Even after her betrayal, Val could not bring himself to do it. He had heard that women's prisons were no joke, that they were even worse than men's prisons. Robin was a young gal, a few years younger than himself. Combined with drug charges she would certainly have gotten at the time had the cops investigated her, there was no way she would have avoided prison.

"Oh... that. You don't have to thank me for that." Once again, he picked at his food. It was the only way he could keep from looking her in the eye and not make it too obvious. She still knew, but it didn't matter.

"I do. And also, I figured this was a good opportunity to apologize for what I did." His eyes lifted from his plate, and aligned with hers. "I wish I never met that jackass."

"That right? Then why'd you stay with him all this time?" Val immediately regretted asking that question. He knew the type of man William Cook was. The word 'man' was inappropriate. William, being the controlling type, likely scared Robin into remaining in the relationship. "I'm sorry. Don't answer that."

"It's alright. Wouldn't have happened had I not been so stupid."

"So, why now?" Val asked. "You said you broke up with him today. What made you do it?"

"Well, of course there was his behavior at the Bowen's place. But more importantly..." she smiled nervously. She looked away, only to turn her gaze back to him. "It was seeing you again." She embraced the image of Valentine Krane with her hands, as though beholding the sight of a game show prize. "Look at you. You're... completely different. You look healthy. You're running a business. From what I gather, you seem to be doing really well."

A warm smile creased Val's face. "I'm doing alright. There's a good man I have to thank for that."

"Even though our reacquaintance... let's just say, went sideways... just by looking at you, I could tell that you changed. That you were happier. I guess, that was the straw that broke the camel's back. I wanted that for myself."

"Good." He smiled enthusiastically. "Good! I'm seriously happy for you." All of a sudden, the crappy feeling that plagued him all day was gone. Perhaps, the misery he endured had happened for a reason. "So, what's next for you? Going back home?"

"Eh, I'm thinking I might wait. Seeing as William and I share an address, and considering how I dumped him off on the side of the road…"

"I see. Good point," Val said. "You planning to stay in town?"

"I'm thinking that's best."

"There's some motels around the corner."

"Yeah, I drove past them." Her voice was sullen, as was her body language.

Val studied her expression, sensing something else was wrong. "You… have money for a motel?"

She pursed her lips, embarrassed at the revelation. "Like I said, I'm working, but it barely covers all of the expenses. Then I had to buy that dress and drive all the way out here." A groan followed the statement.

It came as no surprise that William Cook provided no income. With this new information, piecing together Robin's predicament was easy.

"They were gonna let you stay at the lake house. You weren't anticipating shoveling eighty-bucks a night for room and board."

Robin cracked another smile. "I thought *I* was supposed to be   the   detective."

Two inner voices argued in Val's mind. There was heated contention between his compassionate side, which was eager to help, and his pessimistic side, which warned him to keep his mouth shut and let her figure this out for herself.

Ten minutes ago, that pessimistic side would have won. But now, Val could not help but study her gorgeous features. Her eyes were hazel, her skin kissed by the sun, her teeth white as heaven, gifting the world with a perfect smile.

"Oh, before I forget." Robin leaned over and reached into her bag. From it, she pulled out the circuit breaker and wires which he had left at the Bowen's property. "Thought I'd return those to you."

"Jesus, thanks," he said. "Not a huge deal. Just a couple hundred bucks worth of equipment, but still, I certainly appreciate it."

That perfect smile took form. "You're welcome."

In that moment, the compassionate side officially won.

"Listen... I have a spare room at my place. There's a bed, nice and comfy. You can stay there until you figure things out. No strings attached, no funny business."

Another smile. "Really?"

"Yeah. Really."

"You know, I think I'll take you up on that. If it's not too much trouble."

He shook his head. "None at all."

The pessimistic side of his brain screamed at him. *You dumb idiot.*

The opposite side intervened. *You're doing a good thing. Look at how happy and grateful she is.*

Robin finished her plate and stood up. "You want me to just follow you to your place?"

"Yeah." Val stood up and dug for his wallet. "Go ahead and head out. I'll pay at the front counter."

"Alright." She gave him a brief, but affectionate look, then went out. Val caught himself watching her, admiring her figure along the way.

No, no, dummy. Nothing like that is gonna happen. Damn, it's been so long since you've been with someone, you're actually contemplating that possibility. He physically shook his head to rid himself of the thought.

"You said it yourself. No strings attached," he muttered. He went to the counter to pay the bill.

This time, he couldn't have cared less about the people staring at him.

CHAPTER 8

Val led the way, guiding Robin through a couple miles of road covered by thick canopy. The area around the lake was heavily wooded and often filled with campers. Often, especially in the evening, he made sure to slow down due to hikers who were obscured in the shadows. Tonight was no different. Two ladies, both in their later twenties, carrying camping gear on their backs, were waiting by the tree line waiting for them to pass.

It was the perfect time of year for hiking and camping. The forecast called for nothing but sunshine for the rest of the month. The lake provided plenty of coves for those who wanted to camp by the lake. With the exception of a few properties near the end, the south half of the lake was vacant.

Val slowed and watched his mirror. After he and Robin passed by, the two ladies crossed the road and disappeared into the woods. South it was, where they were likely hoping to find some privacy.

He grinned, then followed the trail another hundred yards to his residence. Robin parked her vehicle alongside his, then stepped out to gaze at the lake.

"Oh, wow. This is heaven."

Val stood beside her, sharing her appreciation for nature's serenity. "Yeah, I think so."

Robin took in the sight of the property. The house held two-thousand square feet of space. It had a patio overlooking the lake, with an awning for shade. In the middle of the front yard was a bench facing a firepit stocked with dry wood. There were trees on both side of the property, with a little space near the shore which allowed a little trail to the neighbor's house. At the dock was a small paddleboat and a twelve-foot aluminum boat.

"Jesus, Val. It's like you're a completely different person."

"You can say that." He took her bag and took it into the house for her. "In some ways, I'm the same."

"You're not still using, are you?"

"Hmm?" He realized she was referencing the few times he smoked meth during those years of bad decisions. "Oh. Hell no." He pointed at the water. "I was referring to water skiing. Don't you remember? Lake Treasure?"

Robin smiled. "How could I not?"

Even at the height of their time as low-life bums, there were some genuinely good memories to be treasured. One of which was at Lake Treasure, where they met up with a friend who owned a speedboat.

Robin started laughing. "Oh man, I'm surprised you're willing to bring that up."

He chuckled. "You're the only one here, so I guess it's less embarrassing. Nothing you hadn't seen before."

"Not like that, though," she said. "Not every day you see your boyfriend catch a wave, completely flip over and lose his shorts in a nosedive."

"Oh geez." He shut his eyes, reliving the event in his memory. "To this day, I still wonder what happened to my trunks. I thought they would float up."

Robin laughed harder. "We were at the back of the boat watching you look around, like 'what the fuck?' We weren't sure what the problem was until Marvin brought the boat over to you. You were like 'Hold on! Hold on!' Then Baker realized what happened, pointed down and…" She doubled over, unable to contain her fit of laughter.

For her amusement, Val finished the story on her behalf.

"Yeah, that prick." He mocked his old acquaintance, pointing at the water, completely amused. "'I see his ass! Look at that everybody. I see his ass! His shorts are gone!' Jackass just *had* to point it out for everyone."

Robin was tearing up. "Not like we weren't gonna notice when you stepped aboard."

"Yeah. I totally remember the "common courtesy" I received when everyone *watched* as I stepped aboard, completely bottomless."

"Hey. Shouldn't have taken them off."

"I didn't take them off! I hit the water at an angle. Lake Treasure took them off. And hid them. The bastard." Shaking his head, he unlocked the door and let them in.

Robin followed him in, taking a moment to appreciate the layout. There was a nice round living room and fireplace. Further back, a counter divided the kitchen from the living room. There was an island in the middle of the kitchen, and to add charm to it, Val had a little fountain in the middle with a palm tree. At the back of the kitchen was a hallway which led to the utility room, basement, and bedrooms.

She followed him through the kitchen and into the hall. On the lefthand side was an empty room.

"I hope this'll be comfortable for you."

She went in and tested the bed. Memory foam. "This is great. Thank you, Val."

"I need a beer. You want one?"

"Sure." She followed him into the kitchen. "Wow. This beats any Bed and Breakfast I've ever been to."

"How many have you been to?" he said.

"Not a lot."

"Considering your roommate, I'm not too surprised." He reached into the fridge and pulled out two beer bottles. "On that note, I need to ask: do you feel like you might be in danger? You need to speak with the police?"

The thought of William was a draining one. She accepted a beer from Val, then returned to the living room. Sinking into the sofa, she stared at the bottle while contemplating all the clean-up that lied ahead. That was the issue with messy breakups, especially between live-in couples.

"I'll give him a call tomorrow or the next day and let him know what's up."

"You think he's still in town?" Val asked.

"I have no idea," she replied. "He had s couple buddies he hangs out with. And by hanging out, I mean go to bars, drink incessantly and smoke meth, among other stupid things."

"Sounds about right."

"Yeah. A big guy named Barker... don't ask... and a skinny drug addict dipshit named Dustin. You'd see him a mile away thanks to his tattoos. My guess is that he called them for a pickup. If he made the call right after I ditched him, then they should've arrived by this afternoon. Either they went straight home, or decided to remain in town for a while."

"Alright." Already halfway through his beer, he joined her in the living room.

Robin was already draining hers. She leaned to her left to admire the water through the window.

"It's beautiful here."

"Sorry to hear about the wedding," Val said. "From what I saw, it looked like a beautiful setup. Is the ceremony supposed to take place by the water?"

"Yeah." Robin was disinterested. "I don't care anymore. Let the bitch have her stupid party. God help Dale for marrying her."

Val rocked in his chair, studying her facial features. "You sure you're alright?"

She looked at him and smiled. "I'm more than alright."

"Yeah? Mind if I ask why?"

She scooted to the end of the sofa nearest to him. "Well, they say to better your life, you need to kick out the toxic elements. For some people, that's drugs or alcohol. For me, it was people. Leslie booted me, but now that I've cooled off on the matter, I realize she did me a favor. Then I kicked William out of my life—something *long* overdue. Then I found you again."

It had been many years since Val felt the nervous thrill of butterflies in his stomach. He tried to play it cool, while internally debating whether he wanted to entertain the ideas which were clearly going through her head. Judging by the way those eyes were looking at him, there was no mistaking her intent.

"Is that why you searched all over town for me?"

"So what if it was?" She placed her bottle down on a side table, then leaned on the arm of the sofa. "It's been a long time since I've seen you. I guess I missed you more than I thought."

She reached and touched his arm.

Val watched her hand stroke his bicep. "You sure this isn't just a rebound thing? We've only been reacquainted for like, I don't know, an hour? And let's not forget *why* you and I are no longer a thing."

Robin withdrew and leaned into the back cushion. "I can't blame you for holding that against me. If it makes you feel better, it's been a miserable ten years."

Val immediately regretted bringing it up. "No, it does not make me feel better." He finished his beer, then returned to the kitchen. He returned with two more beer bottles. Instead of taking a seat, he went for the door. "You know what would?"

"What's that?"

"Being outside, watching the lake, with a warm fire."

She looked out the window at the firepit. "Sounds… romantic." A white smile graced her host.

"Better to do it while we have some sunlight left," he said.

"Then what are we waiting for?" she said. She was out the door in a flash.

Val grinned. There was still that voice in the back of his mind warning him about how fast this was going. Still, he couldn't help but proceed. Maybe this could be the start to something good. Maybe, just maybe, he and Robin could experience a healthy relationship for a change.

Besides, what better revenge was there than stealing the girl back from William Cook?

That thought alone made a night with Robin worth it.

CHAPTER 9

This cove was a good place. It was near the water, but had a few trees to obscure any peeping toms who wanted to sneak by on a boat. Beyond those trees was a small clearing in the woods, providing level ground for a tent as well as a campfire. Their proximity to lapping water and the frogs croaking provided leisure to the two hikers as they set up camp for the night.

Even with the cover of night, Camryn could not stop looking around. The incident at the cove had made her anxious. Having been seen by those fat jerks, she now felt there was always a set of eyes on her at all times. The woods provided obscurity, not only for them, but for any peepers who may be watching. She knew her concerns were a tad pretentious. They were on the southern half of the lake. For the most part, the only other humans here were other campers and boaters. Any fishermen on boats would not be able to spy on them from the lake thanks to the thin grove of trees at the water's edge.

Camryn's partner, Jo, was knelt at the campfire. The flame had finally spread to the wood and was steadily climbing. Camryn appreciated the way the fire illuminated her figure. Her love for hiking was evident in her tan, muscular legs and arms. During the summer, Jo constantly arranged walks at the park, or camping trips. Exploring the woods brought endless adventure.

This active lifestyle took a couple of years to grow on Camryn, but eventually it did. There was more to life than going to bars, restaurants, and movie theaters. She was the average girl, while Jo was the adventurer. In the beginning, Camryn complained. Why did they need to leave the house so much? In her opinion, going to work took enough of her time. Over the course of time, after seeing new places, that attitude changed. In the process, she lost fifteen pounds and gained a muscle tone she never thought she would ever see on herself. It was certainly more than she ever would achieve at the gym, which she only visited once every three weeks at best.

Jo fixed her brunette hair and looked over at her. "You hungry?"

"Surprisingly, no. The trail mix seems to be tiding me over," Camryn said. She stood by the trees at the cove's edge, watching the moon's reflection on the lake. "It's beautiful here."

Her girlfriend laughed. "There's nobody coming."

Camryn put her hands over her chest. The thought that those disgusting pricks were probably getting their rocks off by watching them was sickening. On the other hand, she felt stupid for letting Jo seduce her in broad daylight, out in the open. She succumbed to the heat of the moment, and tapped into an adventurous side she didn't know even existed.

"I'm just watching the lake."

"It is beautiful," Jo said. She laid a blanket down and sprawled over it. "Today was fun."

"For the most part."

"Oh, it'll give us something to laugh about in the future. Besides, it's not like they saw *all* of you."

"Thank God," Camryn said. She could only imagine how frantic she would have been had she and Jo gotten around to removing their undergarments.

Jo leaned to the fire and rubbed her hands. The summer was hot, but the warmth of a blazing campfire was always a relaxing sight. The wood crackled and popped, the smoke lifting into the canopy.

Jo rested on her elbow and leaned up to look at Camryn. "Why don't you come over here?"

"I'm admiring the lake."

"You're watching for peeps."

Camryn sighed. "So what if I am?"

"What is there for them to spy on? You look dressed to me." She cracked a smile. "Or are you suggesting that'll change once you come by the tent?"

"Knowing you..." Camryn tucked her chin down, pretending to be shy. Jo was always the 'dude' in this relationship, always making advances and coming to Camryn's side of the bed. Camryn always played the role of needing to be charmed.

"Knowing me what?" When her partner didn't answer, Jo decided to stand up and walk over.

Camryn's act broke when she felt warm hands stroke her shoulders, the fingertips pushing under her tank top straps. Lips touched the back of her neck. Finally, Jo went for something more affectionate by giving her a tight hug from behind. Camryn put her hands on hers and leaned her head back, pressing her cheek to Jo's.

"I know what you're up to."

Jo mimicked astonishment. "I have no idea what you're getting at."

"Oh, shut up."

Jo giggled and began kissing her neck. Her hands broke the hug and went to searching Camryn's body, ready to pick up where they left off earlier that day.

Camryn closed her eyes and respired, letting the ecstasy overtake her. No amount of booze or weed could amount to the high she got from Jo's touch. Her hands were under her shirt now, exposing the tan flesh underneath.

She opened her eyes, turned, and pressed her lips to Jo's. They took their activities back to the tent.

****

The fire crackled in front of them, the flickering flames creating a soothing atmosphere. The water gently lapped. In the distance, a loon called out. Near the shore, crickets and frogs had begun their nightly chorus.

Val and Robin sat on the wood bench, beers in hand. Robin was already on her third, reminiscing about the last ten years.

"Most nights, I sleep on the couch. The nights I'm home, I do, anyway. Often I try to pick up night shifts whenever I can. I needed the money, and frankly it kept me out of the house, away from his drug use. When I was at home, I was just under his control. So I got by. Cooked him meals, paid the bills, did the bare minimum in sex."

Val flinched at that uncomfortable thought. Over the past half-hour, she detailed the history of her life since he went to prison. At this point, he wasn't sure which of them had it worse.

"He was like that since the beginning, wasn't he?"

Robin played with her beer bottle. "Yep." Down the rest of it went. "I wish I could've gotten away sooner. Could've spared myself almost a decade of misery. But, I was afraid. Still am, to be honest. People like William make you too scared to leave. You're always afraid of how they'll react, especially when their brain is fried with coke."

"Why the hell did you dump me for him, then?"

She looked over at him. "Is that a serious question?"

Val watched the fire, reminiscing over his own past. "No, that's a dumb question. Basically you traded one loser for another. Though I must say you go for a type. Drug addicted, unemployed losers, who cheat and steal their way through life."

"I was younger then."

"We were both younger then," Val said. "We were old enough. We knew right from wrong."

"The difference now is that doing right sounds more appealing," Robin said. She scooted closer to his side of the bench. "I couldn't believe it when I saw you. I never would've guessed this was you. I imagine being here, in this place, helps a great deal."

They admired the beauty of the lake together.

"Yeah, there's something about this place," Val said. "It's nice in winter too. The lake freezes over just enough to hold onto the snow. The ducks swim in the thawed sections. When I'm not working, I sit in the living room with the fireplace going."

"That sounds cozy."

"It is."

"You, uh…" Robin grinned like a shy high school girl. "You have anyone to share that coziness with? Some small town country girl? There's a few pretty ones that live around here."

"That there are," he said with a smile. "But no. Though I get along with everybody, my reputation ended up following me here. Nobody wants to hook up with an ex-con. Part of the reason I have a stable business is because I frequently have to drive out of town."

"You ever wish to share all of this with someone?"

Val looked at her, easily reading between the lines. "Gosh, you're moving quick, aren't ya?" She shrugged and smiled, not debating that fact at all. "You just kicked a boyfriend of ten years to the curb, and already you're keen on hooking up? Is this a rebound sort of thing?"

"I might've shared a house with William for ten years, but as far as I see it, I've been alone most of that time," she said. "You pointed out how I used to be attracted to losers. Well, that's one way I've matured. I've been craving a winner lately. And, by the way, I'm not looking for a hookup. I'm looking for something healthy and permanent."

She took the initiative, cupping Val's face with both hands, and pressing her lips to his. His hands rose up in surprise, but did not push her away. The touch of her lips was as soothing as the sounds of crackling fire and splashing water.

One kiss led to another, then another, then another. Robin swung herself around, straddling her host. She pressed her forehead against his and smiled.

"Nobody around here gets you, but I do." She ran her finger down his chest. "What do you say? You willing to give me a shot while I'm here?"

Val wrapped his arms around her waist. The woman knew what she was doing and it was working. Val had his reservations, but could not deny the basic facts.

He answered by resuming the kissing session. Hands gripped fistfuls of clothing, buttons ripped, sandals kicked off... falling right into the flames.

Robin looked back and laughed. "Oh, no!" She dropped her forehead to Val's shoulder.

He laughed with her. "I'll buy you new ones."

Once again, they were back at it. Val wrapped his arms under Robin's thighs and carried her into the house. Blinded by the dark and Robin's vigorous kissing, he quickly lost his footing, tripping over the edge of the carpet.

Down to the floor they went. The carpet folded, their feet bumping into the side-table, knocking it over and shattering the picture frame propped atop of it. Both lovers descended into a fit of half-drunken laughter before grabbing one another.

There was no point in relocating. The living room floor would suffice.

****

The air was hot and misty, the two bodies in the tents acting as furnaces. As instructed by her lover, Camryn remained perfectly still, allowing Jo to work her magic. She was on her back, hands over her head, clutching heartily at the balled up blankets. All reservations about being bare in the woods were gone, seized by the overwhelming power of ecstasy.

All she could hear beyond her own heavy breathing was that of Jo. Lying on her stomach further down, toes tapping the side of the tent while she worked on Camryn.

A splash of water in the distance made Camryn open her eyes. She raised her head, looking down the length of her naked body at Jo. The tent behind her was lit orange by the fire outside.

"Did you hear something?"

Jo didn't even bother lifting her head. "Shut up, babe."

Camryn leaned up on one hand and pointed. "But I heard…" Jo seized her wrist and pinned it the ground. She quickly grabbed Camryn's other hand and did the same, planting them by her hips and holding them there while she resumed her work.

The use of force sparked a new wave of pleasure. Camryn accepted her fate and allowed herself to be dominated. In the course of the next minute, things went back to normal. She shifted side to side as the buildup within her neared its natural conclusion.

Thump. Thump. Thump.

At first, she thought her paranoia was trying to ruin her good time. She closed her eyes and reminded herself that nobody was out there, and to not let her imagination ruin what was looking to be a hell of an orgasm.

Thump. Thump. Thump.

They sounded like footsteps of sorts, carrying something large. Again, it was faint enough to assume it was her overactive imagination. The fact that Jo didn't seem to pick up on it helped put Camryn at ease. Then again, how could she hear with Camryn's legs squeezing her head?

The finale was reached, and Camryn called out, her fingernails digging into the tent floor. Ripples of pleasure streamed through her body, gradually weakening, leaving her feeling like an empty husk.

Jo lifted her head and sat up, pleased with the results of her work. "See what happens when you stop worrying?"

Camryn slowly caught her breath. "Yeah."

"Nothing here but you and me, baby."

Camryn finally opened her eyes to look at her sweetheart. Behind her was a dark shadow eclipsing the fiery glow. It was almost as wide as the tent entrance. Above it was the shadow of what appeared to be a massive king cobra. Two elongated 'jaws' protruded from the appendage. They were long and pointed, and angling toward the tent.

Camryn pointed and screamed.

There was no time for Jo to turn and look. The thing tore through the polyester and planted right on her shoulder. As the serrated edged claw shut over her flesh, a second one ripped through the tent, grabbing her by the waist. Jo screamed, thrashing in the grip of an enormous crab.

Like a massive spider, it backed away, dragging its writhing victim toward the water.

"JO!" Camryn screamed. She ran to the breach in the tent, just in time to see her lover get pinned to the ground. The crab was holding her down with one claw, using the other to surgically open her abdomen. Jo gagged and convulsed with every foot of intestine that was pulled from her body.

The thing had no regard for the pain it caused. It scooped her innards into its mouth as casually as a child eating spaghetti at the dinner table. The shock of seeing her lover being eaten alive, and the sheer terror of her killer, blinded Camryn to the presence of a second crab—until it was in her face.

It darted in from the right, widening the gash in the tent made by its predecessor. Camryn fell backwards, then scampered on her palms and heels to the back of the tent. The creature tore the wall open with ease, then pressed inward. Pincers, black in color with pasty-white tips, extended toward her.

For a split-second, she thought she was looking at the paws of a huge black bear. The claws seemed to be covered in thick patches of fur. Only when the white-tipped pincers opened did it become clear this thing was a monster crab.

"No! No! Get away!"

Lost in a fit of panic, she kicked at the thing. For the crab, she may as well have been offering her feet. It seized her by the ankle, instantly snapping the bone.

Screaming in agony, Camryn was pulled closer. For the second time, she was on her back, hands gripping the blankets tightly.

The crab plunged the tips of its other claw into her ribcage and proceeded to peel her apart. It ripped chunks of meat and bone and delivered them to the mandibles. Like its brethren, it held no concern for the agony it caused. The luxury of death took its sweet time, forcing Camryn to experience having her stomach and liver removed before slipping away.

Another joined in, thrashing the tent in hopes of finding a third human. After its found nothing, it turned to the fresh kill on the ground and reached for one of the arms. Its brethren sprang, determined to protect its kill.

The straggler scurried back, unwilling to match the ferocity of the other. It then made its way to the other crab feeding past the campfire, only to get a similar violent result. These crabs were not willing to share.

With no other sign of prey here, the straggler returned to the waters in search of new meat.

It traveled north within the shallows, until another orange flickering light caught its attention. There was another habitat, this one larger and sturdier. Since entering this lake, the creatures had learned that such structures were often occupied by humans.

With no other crabs around to impede its hunt, the crustacean took the initiative and eased into the shallows.

****

It was a passion that was simultaneously old and new. Their spark, doused by years of bad decisions, had reignited into a blazing hot fire. Any reservations Val had felt beforehand were quickly overridden by renewed affection and physical desire.

They held each other tightly as their shared pleasure reached its peak. Val dropped his head to her shoulder, smelling the fruity fragrance. They took a moment to recover, after which they looked at each other and laughed. In their clumsy, drunken enthusiasm, they had practically wrecked the living room. Val didn't care. Picture frames could be replaced, the table could be fixed, and everything else straightened. Right now, he was riding the high of winning the girl back.

"I guess something good came from your ex-friend's wedding," he said.

"I'd say so." Robin smiled and tapped his face. Finally, she eased him off. Now that the heat of their embrace had worn off, she was starting to feel a tad chilly. She laughed as she searched in the darkness for her clothes, which had been yanked off and tossed away without care.

Val stood up and went to the kitchen. Robin laughed at the sight of him, naked, filling the coffee pot.

"You just gonna freestyle it?" she said. "This a new thing you picked up since moving here?"

"Maybe it is," he replied. "Nah. Now that it's dark, I'm just planning on throwing on a t-shirt and sweats once I'm done here. Right now, I'm in need of coffee."

Robin found her clothes and pulled them on. "Well, good sir, I'll be out at the dock admiring the water. Once you're all set, would you be so kind to bring me a mug?" She eyed his naked body. "And if you wanna bring it out like that, I won't complain."

"Maybe I will," he said with a smile. "Neighbor's gone. Nobody around to notice. Nobody but you." He winked then began filling the pot with water.

Robin returned the gesture. Floating in bliss, she trotted outside, smiling ear-to-ear. She had defeated her demon and regained her angel in a single day. It was storybook-level romance, something many of her peers would balk at, but it was real. Robin did not concern herself with the speculation others would have regarding this change of events. If things went well, and she and Val managed to do things right this time, she would hopefully move out here with him.

She stepped by the campfire, seeing her shoes smoldering with the logs. *Yeah, those are goners. Worth the sacrifice, though.* She put a couple more logs in the pit, then went to the edge of the dock.

The lake was still and glassy, perfectly reflecting the moonlight. It was a mesmerizing sight. She sat on the edge and put her feet in the water. The temperature was perfect. Had there not been coffee brewing, she would consider going for a swim. The thought sparked new ideas, all of which brought a smile to her face. Her newfound happiness made her feel adventurous. Under the cover of night, she and Val could enjoy a 'special' swim.

Such things would wait for later. Right now, Robin chose to settle for what she had. She stroked the water with her feet, listening to the loons calling from somewhere across the lake. Bugs hopped across the water, one of them being an unlucky meal for a fish. The fire behind her crackled. In the house, Val was digging through the cabinets, ready to join her with some late night brew.

Robin looked down, watching her feet in the water. "Thank you God, for this perfect night."

Sudden pain stripped Robin of her bliss and put her in a world of terror. A huge claw, like garden shears, reached from the water and shut over her ankle. Panic, pain, and confusion hit her at once. She could feel the edge of the pincer clamping over her bone.

She fell back against the dock, her legs still hung over the side. More pain surged through her body, for another white-tipped claw had reached up and sliced into her. There was a sensation of tugging and the wood dock scraping against her back. Her attacker, whatever it was, was pulling her into the water.

She was pulled over the edge of the dock, where she free-fell into the water.

Screaming Val's name, Robin rolled to her stomach and reached up to grab something, anything. She found the leg of the dock and pulled herself up, spitting warm lake water.

She held on for dear life, everything below her shoulders still submerged. The thing continued to pull, each movement resulting in fresh lacerations to her thigh and calf. She felt like a string being tugged by something with blades for hands.

"OH GOD! VAL! HELP!"

Val heard the screams and the splash. He ran to the door and peered out to see what was happening. Robin was in the water, nearly obscured by his aluminum boat.

Whatever was happening, it was drastic, and did not give him the time to pull on some pants. He ran out to the dock, dropping to his knees at the edge. Robin's jaw was fully extended, her eyes bulging from ungodly pain.

He reached down. "Grab my hand! Robin just grab—" The lake exploded, the submerged attacker showing its ugly face as it turned its attention on him. Its bulky, disc-shaped body broke the surface. Huge claws, covered in fur, snapped shut within a couple centimeters of his face.

Val yelled and fell back.

Immediately, he had to battle against the confusion that came with the creature's presence. There was no question what it was he just saw. The body, the eyestalks, the legs, the pincers—it was a giant crab.

Robin, having been released from its grip, tried to swim to shore. "Val, help me!"

He rolled to his hands and knees, spotting her in the water on the left side of the dock. Blood loss and shock blinded her, making her wade right into the twelve-footer.

"Robin! Turn to your left. Reach for my hand! I'm right here!"

Gasping for breath and tearing up, she turned and spotted him. She reached out, her hand grasping for his.

Almost there, just another inch or two…

The water erupted again. The crab rammed Robin with the force of three defensive linebackers, driving the back of her head into the bow of the twelve-footer. Blood and hair splattered onto the hull.

Stunned, Robin was unable to do anything but take the imminent punishment.

"NO!" Val screamed, his hand still outstretched.

There was nothing he could do. The crab hacked at her, plunging the white tip of its pincer though her eye socket, then ripping it out the side, leaving her skull broken like a cracked egg. It proceeded to hack away at her, exposing her stomach tissue with a few quick movements. Limbs fell away, blood filled the water, and in a few quick moments, Robin was completely unrecognizable.

Val scrambled to his feet and ran to the house. The phone! He needed the phone! It was on the kitchen counter, across the living room. He entered the house, took a step in, and for the second time that night, tripped over the edge of the carpet.

He was unconscious as soon as he hit the floor.

CHAPTER 10

The night was easier on Taylor Davies this time. She enjoyed a long, deep sleep, which was eventually broken by her alarm clock. After the dreaded first ten minutes of waking up, her energy returned, and she found herself in a much better mood than yesterday.

If Taylor appreciated anything in life, it was going to work without a headache. There was no medical reason for her semi-frequent onsets, they just came on whenever she was tired or stressed.

Good weather also had a positive effect on her mood. This Friday morning was a beautiful one. The sun was out, bringing out the green in the trees. There was a mild breeze in the air, keeping the temperature at a perfect seventy-eight. There was less traffic than yesterday. With a little luck, there would be no altercations requiring her intervention.

Even Alan Goldstein wasn't as aggravating today as he sometimes could be. During their morning patrol, they had a decent chit-chat about his annoying aunt who was due to come into town next week.

Driving one-handed, Taylor cruised the streets, chuckling at the account of Alan's misery.

"Fast-forward to last week. We get this group text. My dumb niece—I love her, she's very sweet, but she's dumb as a brick—got engaged to her boyfriend. Keep in mind, she's only known this guy for seven months, broke up twice during that time, and he has a seven-month old daughter from another relationship."

"Oh, geez," Taylor said. "Certainly a recipe for success. How old is she again?"

"She'll be nineteen in a couple of months."

"Fabulous."

"Right? So, my cousin sends out the group text—and by the way, I fucking hate group texts—and she's asking for us to send love and support. I'm thinking, no freaking way. I don't give false support for dumb decisions, so I don't bother responding. A day or two later, my cousin texts me directly, and asks me to say congratulations to her kid. I, being a little too honest sometimes, say no, and give my reasons."

"Let me guess: you're the bad guy?"

"Yep. Then I get a text from my stupid aunt, telling me how cold I am. You can imagine how excited I am for her to come into town next week. She and my mother will probably try and double-team me on this issue."

"Just don't go to your mom's place. Claim you have overtime."

Alan smiled. "Well, you know how much I like picking up extra hours."

"I do," Taylor said, smirking. "That's why I know you can afford to buy me a coffee."

"Buy *you* a coffee?"

"Oh, don't play dumb. I picked up the last three tabs, you mooch. It's your turn." She steered the vehicle into the parking lot of the Pine Tree Café. "Or I might have to message your mother about how excited you are to attend your niece's wedding."

Alan shot her a stern look. "You wouldn't. You *couldn't*. You don't have her number."

"Oh, hush. She friended me on Facebook after she brought cupcakes to the station."

"Oh… right." Alan stepped out. "Alright. Come get your coffee."

Taylor slammed her door shut and pranced to the front entrance. "And a donut."

"Classic cop," he said, chuckling. "Geez, you're in a good mood today."

"Slept like a baby. Don't do anything to ruin it," she said. She stepped into the café and went to the counter.

The clerk turned to her and smiled. "Hi, Taylor. Coffee with two sugars?"

"And a strawberry donut. I'll earn it later at the gym," she said.

The clerk chuckled and looked at Alan. "What about you?"

"I need to get my membership going again," he said. "That said, I'll keep my calories down and just get a black coffee. No sugar, no pastries."

The clerk pointed at the donuts at the end of the bottom row. "We have vegan pastries." Alan's visible disgust got a laugh out of her. "Just the coffee, then." She put on her plastic gloves and went to work. She bagged the donut and handed it to Taylor. "Hey, I have a question for ya?"

"What's that?" Taylor said.

"You guys responded to that thing at the Bowens' property, right? The one where Valentine Krane got into a fight with his ex-girlfriend."

Alan stepped forward. "That's right."

"Well…" Taylor paused, unsure if it was worth explaining that the situation was more complicated than a beef between old flames.

"They were here yesterday," the clerk said. "I was waitressing last night, and Mr. Krane was in. Then she was here, and whenever I arrived at their table, it looked pretty tense."

"Were they fighting?" Alan said.

"From what I saw, they didn't look pleased. Then they got up and left at the same time. A few other customers said it looked like they were having an argument. All I can say is she looked really uncomfortable."

"She showed up after he did?" Taylor asked.

"That is true, but when she arrived, she didn't appear like she was looking for a fight. I don't know, I just thought it might be worth bringing up, since the situation at Arthur Bowens' place got pretty violent. From what I hear, that is."

Alan paid for the items, then took his coffee. "Thanks for letting us know. Maybe we'll swing by Val's place and do a follow-up." He stepped outside, not giving his partner any chance to give her objection in public. At first, it did not seem like a big issue, until Taylor saw him get into the driver's seat.

"What are you doing?"

"We have a case."

"No we don't."

"Isn't it in Ms. What's-her-name's best interest for us to check in?"

"They were in separate vehicles, Alan. It's not like he snatched her up and hauled her into the woods." Taylor stood at the driver's side window. She snapped her fingers at Alan's face. "Out. You know the deal. *I* drive."

He stuck his tongue out at her like a rebellious six-year-old. "Make me."

"I'll tase your ass," she said. Alan shifted the vehicle into drive, keeping his foot on the brake. Twice, he eased off of it, threatening to drive off without her. "You're such a child!" She went around to the passenger door and let herself in. Fed up with debating with him, she decided to sip on her coffee.

Alan put his foot to the pedal and steered onto the road. The bump sent hot droplets of coffee splashing right onto Taylor's face.

The look she gave him was nightmare inducing. Alan glanced at her and grinned nervously. "At least none got on your shirt."

Taylor's eyes widened, and she pointed forward. "Light!"

He looked ahead at the red light he was rapidly approaching. "Shit!" He hit the brakes just in time to avoid the rusty pickup truck crossing the intersection.

Coffee splashed upward, popped off the lid, and splattered all over Taylor's shirt.

Taylor looked at her now-brown uniform, then at her partner. The first beads of perspiration were taking form on his head.

"You were saying?"

****

"Stupid assholes," Barker said, raising his middle finger at the cops who almost ran the red. His pal, Dustin, turned the dial up, filling the inside of the truck with rap music. He tossed the butt of his cigarette out the window and lit a fresh one.

The twenty-eight year old turned to his left, revealing his tattooed neck and face to their backseat passenger. "Want one?"

William Cook pulled a cig from the pack and lit it.

Barker turned a left. Up ahead was another motel. He pulled into the driveway and looked at all of the parked vehicles.

"I don't see her car anywhere," he said.

"She's gotta be around here somewhere," William said. He dug out his phone and looked at a text from another associate in his hometown. "Parker just messaged me again. He said she's not at home, not at her mother's place, or at work."

"Does she have any other friends she could be staying with?" Barker said.

"No." William took a puff on his cigarette, then looked at it with contempt. He needed something stronger. Much stronger. "You guys bring any with you?"

Dustin turned again, knowing what 'any' meant. He pulled a little baggie from his pocket and handed it back to William. "Don't hog it all."

William snatched it and immediately snorted some of the white powder. He leaned back in his seat and moaned pleasurably.

"Ohhh. That's better." He whipped his finger over his lip and ran it over his tongue.

"How long you want to keep looking?" Barker asked.

"Until we figure out where that bitch is," William said. "If she never arrived at home, it means she's avoiding me. If she's not at a motel, she's staying with somebody. And I have a feeling I know who that somebody is."

"That ex-boyfriend who beat your ass ten years ago?"

William, high on cocaine and an exploding ego, reached forward and grabbed the subordinate Dustin by the shoulder.

"He did not kick my ass. He jumped me. There's a difference. And that's what we're going to do to him once we find him. You got it."

The tattooed drug addict nodded.

William let him go and inhaled the rest of his cigarette. "Let's keep driving by the residential areas. We'll find him eventually."

"That's fine, as long as you're certain we don't get caught," Barker said.

William's racing mind flashed to what they called the Christopher Leo Incident. It was a night of meth and hot tempers. William had caught Robin laughing with Christopher Leo, a forklift driver from her job. His paranoid mind quickly determined that their chitchat was flirting, and that she was either screwing the guy, or intended to screw him. With the help of Barker and Dustin, he tracked down his residence, and in the dead of night, broke in. Fueled by meth, they beat the poor guy to death.

It was only by pure luck that they were never caught by the police. Their crazed behaviors attracted the attention of a neighbor, a middle-aged woman with a bad back. With their attention on Christopher Leo's bloodied corpse, they did not notice her presence until she peered through the doorway and screamed. William silenced her by smashing a glass bottle over her head, then led a retreat to their truck. By the time another neighbor had stepped out to investigate, they were speeding away. They could hear sirens approaching as they fled the neighborhood.

Robin had suspected William's involvement in Christopher's sudden death, due to his increased use of meth and cocaine during the next few days. A smack to the face silenced her attempt to breach the subject, putting her in her place.

As the weeks went on, the shock of killing another man and severely crippling a woman metamorphosed into jubilation. There was no guilt. Instead, he was buzzing. The cops never traced the crime back to him or his buddies, and to this day, it remained unsolved.

That thrill would pale to that of putting the hurt to Valentine Krane. Ever since their first encounter, William had been itching for payback. In the years since, he took solace in believing Val was getting sodomized on a daily basis.

"He'll be begging for some inmate dick after we're through with him." He thought out loud.

"Huh?" Dustin looked at him. "Wait… what exactly do you plan on doing? We're just beating him up, right? You're not expecting us to…" He mimicked a thrusting action.

"No," William said. Dustin blew a sigh of relief, then faced forward. William watched the window, desperately hoping to spot Robin's car.

Her, on the other hand…

CHAPTER 11

"Just a little more. A little more… keep going… alright!"

Ethan Dowel hit the brakes, then looked out his truck window. The boat was in the water. His nephew Reggie was in the boat, keeping an eye on its distance from the trailer. Once he was certain he was clear, he reversed the boat to make some extra distance, then aligned it with the public dock.

Ethan parked the truck and trailer near some trees, pulled the fishing rods and a cooler out of the bed, then marched to the dock to join his nephew. As soon as his boots touched the wood boards, he heard the annoying ringtone blaring from his pocket.

"Oh, Jesus."

"Aunt Lisa?" Reggie asked.

Ethan handed the rods to his nephew, then looked at his screen. "Yeah." After a brief internal debate, he decided to answer it. "Hey."

"Hey! What did I say? You guys have all day tomorrow to go out on the lake. We have a schedule to keep today, remember?"

Ethan put a finger gun to his temple and mimicked blowing his brains out, much to his nephew's amusement.

"Your company ball isn't until five. It's not even seven-thirty now. We'll be back long before it starts."

"I don't want you guys showing up to this thing smelling like worms and fish!"

"Will you relax? We'll have time to shower before we go. Lisa, we're not sitting around all day in the damn hotel watching paint dry."

"We weren't. Didn't you hear Megan and I when we were talking about going to the art museum?"

"Yes. Reggie and I both heard you. After careful deliberation, he and I decided that we would rather not spend three hours wanting to put an ice pick through our brains, and would rather go to the lake instead."

"Ethan! You're pissing me off."

"What else is new? Listen, your own boss recommended this lake. If we catch something big, we can show him photos. You always complain how I don't mingle with your coworkers during these dinners."

His wife took a few moments to consider his justification. She knew he had no intention of interacting with her colleagues any more than he had to. Still, he was at the lake, and there was nothing she could do to stop that.

"Alright. You guys better be back by two-thirty. We have to be on the road by three-thirty, and I want to make sure you have time to shower and shave."

"Wait? Three-thirty? The thing's not till five!"

"I have to be there early to help set up. I told you this."

"Megan has to be there too?"

"We work for the same company, genius. She's pissed at you for taking Reggie out, by the way."

Ethan shrugged nonchalantly. "So? I've been pissing her off since she was two. I'm actually feeling a bit giddy I found a new way to do it."

"You're a jackass. Alright, have fun. Do. Not. Be. Late. Or I swear, I'll have your balls in a jar."

"Yes honey. I love you oh, so, so, so much. Bye." He ended the call and stuffed the phone in his pocket. As soon as his ass touched the seat, he was starting to bait his hook.

"Where should we go?" Reggie asked.

Ethan looked around. "Let's see… this is the middle part of the lake… the north side is a little busier…" He tilted his head left. "Let's head south. That's what was recommended to me by Lisa's boss."

"South it is."

Reggie turned the boat and accelerated. In this center part of Lake Lucas, there were a few scattered properties on the shore. Behind them was the neck of the lake, which was full of coves.

He began to steer the boat to the right side in search of a good spot. A few hundred feet up was a property with a couple of fishing rods propped at the end of a dock. The folding chair had been knocked over, same with a coffee thermos that was nearby.

Reggie squinted, noticing the oddities in the dock itself. The legs appeared as though a handsaw had been taken to it. Deep grooves, at least an inch thick, marked the wood. The plank at the end was splintered at its center, the two ends uprooted from their nail placements, forming a V-shape.

"The hell happened there?" he said.

Ethan gave it a glance. "Don't know. Looks like someone's in need of repairs," he said. He looked past the dock at the rest of the property. "Truck's there. Shed door's open. Maybe he's about to do some maintenance."

"Maybe he fell," Reggie said. He slowed the boat down. "You think we should check and see if the owner is alright?"

Ethan stood up, gave the dock another quick look, then sat back down. "Nah."

"You sure? If he or she fell into the water, they could be hurt. Or drown."

"Kid, the water's three feet deep at most. Enough to cushion a fall, and unless they landed right on their head, pretty hard to drown in." He pointed to ahead to the left. "Come on. It's not our concern. It's bad enough your mother and aunt are pissed at us. Might as well make this worth it."

Reggie eyed the open shed door, then shrugged. More than likely, the homeowner was in there or in the house.

"Alright." His enthusiasm restored, he sped up.

Ethan pointed ahead and to the left. "Let's head away from this side. Don't want the guy to think we're watching him while he's working."

Reggie steered the boat left, nearing a couple lakefront properties on this side. The first looked like it was having some kind of work done in the yard. There was a long groove near the driveway, either for pipe or cable placement.

The next one looked as though there had been some kind of campfire last night. There was still some smoke lifting from the firepit, with beer bottles scattered in front of the bench.

After this house, there did not appear to be any properties. The entire lake would be fair game. Reggie and Ethan were aware no part of the water was owned by the residents, but they learned never to fish too close to a private dock. On plenty of occasions, they found themselves in an altercation with an angry homeowner, claiming they weren't allowed to cast a line within twenty feet of their dock. It was easier to avoid properties altogether when possible.

Reggie continued on, eyeing a couple coves up ahead.

His uncle stood up, his eyes locked onto the second house's dock. "Wait, wait, wait! Stop the boat. Stop! Stop! Stop!"

Reggie killed the engine. "What's wrong?"

The look on Ethan's face was all the answer he needed. There was not just confusion there, but alarm, for the dock and the bow of the aluminum twelve-footer tied to it were smeared with a brownish red substance. Had it not been for the strands of hair dangling from the rim of the bow, Ethan may had been able to convince himself it was just mud. Maybe the owner ran aground.

But there was no denying reality. He was looking at blood. A lot of blood.

"My brother in Christ." He dug his phone out and dialed 9-1-1. "Yes, I need the cops right away…"

****

Taylor splashed her face with water from the bathroom sink, thinking of all the ways she wanted to murder Alan. She stared at herself in the mirror, watching at her near-naked reflection. Even her bra had been stained by the coffee. Her entire uniform was soiled, forcing her to change completely. Luckily, they had spare shirts and pants in her size available at the station.

After wiping herself down, she began changing into her fresh clothes. A knocking on the door, followed by Alan's voice made her turn around. The guy was already on thin ice. If he was seriously stepping into the women's locker room while she was shirtless, the department would probably have its first murder inside the station.

"Hey! Hurry it up!"

"Dude! You're the reason I'm in here. Don't even think about rushing me."

"We just got a call," he said. His voice was devoid of any humor or sarcasm. "Possible homicide… At Valentine Krane's property."

Taylor quickly buttoned her shirt and pants, strapped on her duty belt, and hurried out the door.

As they walked outside into the lot, her mind began connecting the dots. First the altercation at Bowen's place, then a report of the same two people possibly arguing at the café, and now this. It did not paint a pretty picture.

She got in the driver's seat, then winced. A headache was coming on. So much for having a stressless day.

CHAPTER 12

The nightmare flashed like bolts of lightning, lacking a cohesive narrative for the endless images rushing through his mind. Throbbing pain was like thunder, amplified in the unconscious mind. The screams were distant, then up close, never ending for what felt like an indefinite amount of time.

"Val!"

Robin reached up to him from the water, her fingertips grazing his hand. Her head leaned back, her mouth parting.

"Val!"

The beast emerged from the water. With pincers sharp as secateurs, it slashed at her belly, uncoiling several yards of intestine, and unleashing a fountain of blood. Eyes wide, she shook while her limbs and stomach were torn from the body.

It's pincer reached up and closed over her neck. She closed her eyes and yelled.

"Val!"

"Val!"

He shot up and yelled.

"Whoa! Whoa! Whoa!" someone shouted.

Val felt the breeze coming off the lake, the morning sunlight warming his skin. He looked around, quickly recognizing his driveway and the side of his house. There were cops all around. A couple were on the dock, snapping photos. Another was taking shots of the firepit, while another one stood with a set of tweezers to pull out the burnt flip flops and fabric.

"Val? You okay?"

To his right was Deputy Taylor Davies. He looked down at himself, realizing he was in a stretcher, his naked body covered only by a blanket. He cringed twice, first from humiliation, then from the intense throbbing in his head. The pain and lack of clothing took him back to the horror of the previous night. Like lightning flashes in his mind's eye, he saw Robin screaming, the crab tearing away at her, felt his foot snag on the carpet, and the *thud* of his forehead hitting the floor.

"Where…" He went to bring his hand to his forehead, only for it to stop abruptly. He registered the tightness of a handcuff which chained him to the railing of the stretcher. "What is this?"

Taylor opened her mouth to speak, but remained silent. She broke eye contact, desperately trying to come up with something to say.

Val looked at the cops on the dock. He waved his other hand frantically. "Get away from the water!" They looked in his direction, smirking at his frantic behavior. Their inaction only spurred Val further. He sat up and swung his arm with increased force. "Get off the dock! There's something in the water!"

Everyone stopped what they were doing and looked at him.

Taylor, like the embarrassed relative to a patient with severe mental decline, grabbed him by the wrist.

"Val, stop."

"You don't understand," he said. "There's something…"

"Val, please?"

He realized the blanket had fell away, exposing his lower region. Humiliation blended with shock. Covering himself up, he began to piece together his predicament. His hand was cuffed, detectives and deputies were all over his property, collecting photos and evidence, and none of them had any concern about what was in the water.

One of the deputies stepped out of the house and approached. The tightness in Val's stomach doubled when he recognized Alan Goldstein's face. The guy always had it out for him, convinced he was just another criminal. The look on his face indicated pleasure. Not just any kind of pleasure, but the kind a bully had when he had leverage over someone.

"Oh, good. You're awake," he said. "How's your head?"

Val touched his fingers to his forehead, feeling a bandage.

Alan didn't wait for an answer. He looked at Taylor, holding up a clipboard with a sheet of paper full of handwritten notes.

"The living room is a wreck, they've found burnt flip flops and clothing in the firepit, more clothes in the living room, evidence of violent sexual activity, and…" he looked at the dock, then at Val, "blood on the dock, and on the hull of the boat. They also found hair."

"The hell are you implying?" Val said.

Alan pointed at the car parked beside Val's F-150. "Robin Berry was here last night, wasn't she?"

"Yes."

"Let me guess," Alan said. "You guys had an argument at the diner. You left and came home. Furious, she tracked you down to continue rehashing old wounds. Things got increasingly heated and you snapped. Burnt her clothing, forcibly dragged her onto the living room floor, then finished her off in the lake."

For a moment, Val's vision got so hazy, he thought he was drunk. Never in his life had he ever simultaneously felt so much anger.

"You son of a bitch."

Alan pointed his thumb at the bloody dock. "That's what it's looking like."

"Have you checked my spare room? Her stuff is in there," Val said.

"Doesn't change what we're finding out in front."

"Alan!" Taylor snapped. She glared at her partner with fiery eyes until he backed off. After taking a breath, she turned her attention to Val. "Can you tell us what happened?"

Val barely heard her, for he was distracted by the Sheriff and other deputies who were gathering around him.

"We…" He shut his eyes and clenched his teeth, reliving the horrible events of last night. Though it had been wiped away by the medics, he could still feel Robin's blood on his face and chest.

He looked at the faces around him. Everyone was waiting for him to confess, not bothering to suggest he wait for a lawyer.

"We got together… she went to the dock… I was making coffee… I heard her scream…"

"What happened?" Taylor said.

"She was attacked…"

"By what?" the Sheriff said.

"We found blood on your hands," Alan said.

"I didn't do it!" Val said.

"Then what happened?" Alan said.

"She was attacked by… something?"

"Something?" the Sheriff said. "Mind elaborating?"

"Was it an accident?" Alan said, trying to coax Val into slipping up by disguising the murder as an accident.

Taylor held up her hands. "Whoa! Guys! You know the procedure. He's not officially a suspect yet. After all, we found him unconscious on the floor."

"And evidence of foul play," Alan said.

"He deserves to be consulted by a law—"

"What happened to Robin?" Alan said.

Val sat up suddenly, his eyes bulging, his brow furrowed. "A giant crab got her!"

It sounded as ridiculous as he feared it would. A couple of the deputies had to turn away, failing to suppress their laughter.

"Gentlemen, walk away please," the Sheriff said. The deputies' amusement shifted into embarrassment, their efforts to save face futile as they joined the detectives on the front lawn.

Val looked at the Sheriff, Taylor, and Alan. All three of them had the same awkward body language. Their thoughts were practically broadcasted by their expressions.

"I'm not crazy," he said.

"Nobody said you were," Taylor said. "Sheriff, he took a hard hit on the head. He's clearly…"

"I know what I saw!" Val said.

"A giant crab?" Alan said.

"Deputy?" the Sheriff said. Alan tucked his head and held his hands up, backing away.

The three of them walked a few steps away. Though they spoke under their breath, Val could still pick up what they were saying.

"You can't tell me it's a coincidence Robin Berry gets killed directly after a reported argument with him," Alan said.

"That doesn't mean he killed her," Taylor said. "He's clearly in shock."

"Wouldn't you be after you murdered someone?"

"Alan, get ahold of yourself," Taylor said. "Her truck is in his driveway, her keys and spare clothes in the guest room. It's obvious she was here willingly. Hell, the coffee pot is full. You telling me he brewed a fresh pot before bashing her skull in?"

Alan shrugged. "Considering his history of violence…"

"Oh, give me a break."

Alan tilted his head. "You forgetting he has a criminal history?"

"He's not a psycho."

"Deputies, dial it down," the Sheriff said. He looked at Taylor. "Let's just get him to the hospital and have him looked at by a professional. Personally, I'm more concerned about this nonsense about giant crabs."

"There's blood on the boat too," Alan said. "Maybe he killed her, then lost his mind. Or is pretending he lost his mind."

Listening to this, Val certainly felt like he was about to lose his mind.

"Hey!" he shouted. The three cops turned to look at him. "First of all, if you don't want me to overhear you, walk further away. Second, I didn't fucking kill her!"

"We didn't say you did," the Sheriff said. "I just want a doctor to take a look at you."

"No, you need to search the lake," Val said.

"We will. For the body, unless you can tell us where she is," the Sheriff said.

Val squeezed his fist. The throbbing in his head intensified, as did his heartrate. How could this have happened? Out of nowhere, this demonic thing showed up in his life, killed his old flame, and to make matters worse, the cops were suspecting *him*!

"There's a…" He resisted saying 'giant crab', knowing they would not believe him. "There's an animal in the lake. We came here after meeting at the café, we connected, she went to the dock afterwards… I was inside. I heard her scream. I ran out, and it rammed her against the boat…"

"What kind of animal?" Alan said.

"It was…" Again, Val was not sure if it was a good idea to tell the truth.

One of the detectives approached from the dock. "Excuse me, sir?"

The three cops followed him to the waterline, leaving Val alone on the stretcher.

The paramedics were waiting in the ambulance, with no intention of standing around who they believed to be a cold-blooded murderer.

That headache became unbearable. Val shut his eyes. This was going to be a long day.

CHAPTER 14

In the hour after he phoned the police, Ethan and his nephew Reggie were unsure whether they should remain at the lake. The incident had brought a whole squad of deputies and forensics officers. After giving their statements to the sergeant on scene, they took their boat north, resisting the urge to watch from the water.

There was a feeling of awkwardness. It wasn't every day you stumbled across the scene of a possible homicide. Neither of them were shaken up, but they did feel conflicted about proceeding with their activities.

The two men discussed the issue, leaning toward heading back home. Then Ethan got a text from his wife, stating she was getting ready to go to the museum. All of a sudden, staying on this lake did not sound so bad.

Reggie steered the boat a mile south, eventually settling on a grove of trees that leaned over the water. They were the only ones around so far. It was the middle of the day on a Friday, and most people were still at work. Once it came time to leave, they predicted there would be more people on the lake.

Ethan tossed several casts into the water. Neither the crawler harness nor his crank bait was giving him any luck.

Reggie caught a few small ones with a bobber and hook at twelve inches of depth. The eighteen-year-old was getting bored already. Still, he rather would be bored out here than wandering through the art museum.

"It's the middle of the day," Ethan said. "They've probably gone deeper."

"I'm kinda surprised they didn't go to the shaded area over here," Reggie said.

"That's how it is sometimes," Ethan said.

Reggie sighed. "I guess so." He reeled his line in, then leaned back to stretch. "God, I really don't want to go to that thing tonight."

"You and me both, kid." Ethan checked his watch. "Well, let's move to another spot."

"I saw a little inlet on the left side before we came over here," Reggie said. "It's just a short way up ahead. Wanna try our luck there?"

"Yeah, that's fine," Ethan said. He brought up the bow anchor and sat down. After hoisting the stern anchor, Reggie started the engine back up and steered them to the east side of the lake. Turning forty-five degrees starboard, he pointed the bow directly at the shadowy inlet.

They crossed the lake and arrived at their new spot. Reggie brought the engine down to first gear, easing into the little branch of the lake, which winded like a small river roughly a hundred feet into the landscape.

"Hmm…" Ethan stood up, his eyes on the shoreline.

"See something?" Reggie asked.

"Looks like somebody had a picnic set up here. You see?"

Reggie killed the engine, then stood up. On shore, at the tip of the cove, was a large blanket, partially folded over by the wind. There was a small basket and mini-cooler. Way ahead in the trees was a truck, parked off the trail.

He looked around. "Don't see anyone around. Maybe they went for a walk."

"I don't know." Ethan pointed at the mud on the shore. "See there?"

"The rock?"

"No, not the rock…" Ethan squinted. That was indeed an odd detail. Right there in the water, a couple feet in front of the waterline, was a big, black rock as wide as a patio table. It was smooth, the sides somewhat rough.

Quickly losing interest in the thing, he pointed to the right of it at a group of fresh footprints going into the water.

"Whoever was here, it looks like they were having a good time. Sandwiches and drinks, followed by a little swim…"

"Nobody in the water." Reggie looked around. "Should we find a different spot?"

"No, I'm sick of constantly moving," Ethan said. "Besides, we have to get going soon, or your mother and aunt will crucify me."

"Alright." Reggie dropped the stern anchor. Ethan dropped the bow anchor, tightened it, then snatched his fishing rod. He planted a cast toward the shore on his right, under some outstretched branches.

Reggie moved himself to the middle of the boat, then sent a cast out near the tip of the cove. The crawler harness sank, the water shallower than he expected it to be. His instinct told him there would be no such luck in that spot.

"Ah, dang it." He reeled it back a tad.

"Too far?" Ethan asked.

"Yeah, just a little. Should've aimed about six feet shy—" He stopped, feeling a tug at the end of his line. Excitement sent chills up his spine. Maybe he was wrong...

He froze, waiting for another tug to confirm the presence of a fish, but got nothing. Slowly, he cranked the reel. There was dead weight on the end. His enthusiasm sputtered like air out of a balloon.

"Agh! I snagged something." His uncle laughed at his misfortune. Whatever it was, it wasn't too heavy.

Reggie brought it up to the side of the boat, then burst out with laughter.

Ethan turned around, then joined him. At the end of Reggie's fishing line was a white bra.

"Well, lookie here!" he said. "Looks like our picnic friends might've been having more fun than we thought!"

Reggie looked around. "You think they took their activities to the woods?"

"That, or the truck. Can't really see from here," Ethan said. He reeled his line in and threw a cast close to where Reggie had put his. As he expected, there were no bites. He reeled it in and tried again, same result.

"What are you doing?" Reggie asked. "Trying to dredge the bottom?"

"I'm just curious what else they discarded," Ethan said.

Reggie pried his hook from the bra, then looked at the strap. "Damn. They were playing rough."

"What do you mean?"

"Look at this?"

Ethan looked over his shoulder and saw the torn strap. Frizzy strands of fabric stuck out in all directions. The bra itself did not appear to have been underwater for long. It was still pretty white. It only needed more than a couple hours for the underwater silt to embed itself.

"Some like it rough," Ethan said. "You'll find out once you get into college. Just don't tell you mother I told you that."

Reggie laughed. "Sounds good, Uncle Ethan."

Ethan threw another cast, then reeled it back. This proved to be better amusement than the fishing. If there were any fish in this cove, they probably had been scared away by now due to the incessant number of casts.

The line went taut. Right away, it was clear that it wasn't a fish.

"Oh, boy. What do we have this time?" he said.

"Probably some boxers," Reggie said.

"Ha! No, feels heavier." Ethan reeled the item the rest of the way in, then hoisted it over the bow. "A shoe!"

They both started laughing. Dangling heel up, it looked like an image taken straight out of a cartoon.

"Congratulations," Reggie said. "You think it's a keeper? Should we get a photo with you holding it?"

"Geez." Ethan reached for the line and pulled the shoe close. "The thing's heavy enough, I'll tell you that. I wonder if its full of mud or—AH!" He dropped the shoe, which landed upright on the deck, displaying the stump of the foot still inside.

Reggie jumped back, nearly toppling over the side of the boat. He pointed at the fleshy mound inside, drained of blood.

"Uncle Ethan!"

"I know!" Ethan put a hand on his stomach. "I know…" He looked at the shore, picking up another specific detail. Those footprints on the shore... they were only heading *into* the water.

His mind played a hypothetical scenario. One of them went into the water first, got in trouble, and the other ran in for the rescue, only to get attacked as well. By who?

He thought about the blood on the boat further north.

"Oh, my god. There's a killer on the loose." He grabbed the bow line and started hauling up the anchor. "We're getting out of here. Then we'll call the police again and tell them to come here."

"Where's here?" Reggie said. "What do we tell them?"

"We'll just tell them to look for a cove with a truck, a picnic basket, and a big rock on the shore. Shouldn't be hard to ident—" He looked up, then stiffened with angst.

That rock wasn't there anymore.

He felt something tugging on the anchor line. In the blink of an eye, all weight vanished, leaving behind a coiling rope. Ethan held it up, looked at its frayed end, then turned his eyes to the water.

Just in time to see the big pincers lashing at the boat.

The two arms of the creature clamped on the bow, then yanked down. Water poured over the sides, quickly weighing the small vessel down into the cove.

Ethan and Reggie, confused and taken by surprise, wobbled back and forth, both of them failing to keep their balance. Ethan fell backward, his shoulders landing on the middle seat. Reggie went into the water, flailing with his arms and legs upon impact.

Ethan rolled to his side, the water now completely filling the boat. The bow dipped, causing the stern to rise a few inches.

"Kid?!" He was now in the water. He glanced left and right, gauging the nearest shoreline. Left it was. He kicked and stroked, quickly getting to a point where his feet could touch the bottom. He looked back at Reggie, who had inadvertently backstroked deeper into the lake.

"Kid! Swim over here!" Images of those claws filled his mind. "Get out of the water!"

Reggie spotted him near the trees, gathered his wits, then began swimming toward him.

His arms reached for the sky, and all of a sudden, he began thrashing against his will. Held by his legs, he was pulled back and forth, his mouth open wide. He wanted to scream, but he kept dunking under the water.

The cove turned red.

"Uncle Ethan!" He reared back, arms out. Pincers, like sea serpents emerging around a whaling ship in mythical times, ascended and seized him by the shoulders and neck. They cut flesh and bone with ease, silencing Reggie for all eternity before pulling him under. A hand popped free, reaching straight for the sky.

For a moment, Ethan thought his nephew might have freed himself. That optimism was short-lived. The arm flopped on the surface, the bloody stub that was the shoulder joint jetting bloody water before it sank.

"Oh!" Ethan grabbed his hair, his sanity spiraling into madness. He backed toward the shore, watching the splashing of water where his nephew was being mutilated.

Out of the water, he pulled out his phone. The screen was on, but the case was full of water, causing the touchscreen to not cooperate. He tried bringing up his contacts, but instead the wet screen put on the calendar instead, though the icon was an entire inch away from his thumb.

Giving up, he turned to run into the woods. He only made a single step before noticing the big black rock perched in the shade a couple meters in. The legs expanded and lifted the thing. It turned around, its white-tipped pincers ready for action, its eyes dancing on two black stalks.

Even for a creature its size, it moved with considerable speed, quickly seizing the dumbfounded Ethan Dowel.

He was driven to the ground, flailing his limbs as his entire front was carved open.

Another quickly joined the fray, seizing his forearm and snapping both bones with a single squeeze. It pulled the limb free and fed it into its mandibles. Even in the midst of unworldly agony, Ethan registered the sound of bone crunching in the creature's jaws. Meanwhile, his innards were consumed like warm pasta by the other.

Then there was a buzzing sound, reverberating near his head. He looked over, seeing his phone screen light up. There was Lisa's name, followed by a photo of them at a restaurant table and a small paragraph of text.

Megan and I had a blast. There was a nice restaurant nearby, serving Italian, your favorite. So delicious. Bet you guys wish you didn't go fishing and came with us instead.

CHAPTER 15

"You're free to go. We ask that you don't leave town. There's a good chance we'll need to speak to you further as the investigation proceeds."

Those were the last words spoken to Valentine Krane as he stepped out of the police station. The last several hours were nothing but constant interrogation. The detective on duty was persistent, intensely grilling him with different variations of the same questions in an attempt to trip him up. Val was hit with everything: reports of his and Robin's altercations, reminders of his criminal history, with emphasis on the violent assault, and of course, the odd circumstances surrounding Robin's death.

Had it not been for Robin's truck and belongings at his place, indicating that she was there of her own free will, they would have charged him. As it stood, they did not have enough evidence to hold him. Her belongings were in his spare room, there was evidence of coffee and beer drinking, and the cops did not find a murder weapon. They had checked the boat engine and found that it did not appear to have been used in days.

All they were missing was a body.

Val's mention of a giant crab in the water did not help his case. All it did was garner bemused looks from his interrogators. It quickly became clear that bringing up the creature's existence would do nothing but earn him a night or two at a psychiatric ward. To avoid this, and avoid accusations of altering his story, he referred to the creature as a large animal. After all, it was dark, and everything happened so fast.

He stumbled out of the lot, mentally bruised. The weight of the situation made him feel as if he was being crushed into the pavement. Every time he closed his eyes, he saw those huge pincers pinning Robin to his boat. As though to torture him, his mind concocted different versions of the event, displaying ways he could have saved her. He could have gotten dressed and stepped out right away. He could've grabbed her hand and pulled her up more quickly. Maybe he should have insisted she stay inside. Hell, he should have told her off at the restaurant. It would have been awkward, but at least she would still be alive.

A police SUV pulled up beside him. In the driver's seat was Taylor Davies. She rolled the window down and waved him over to the passenger's seat.

"Get in. I'll give you a lift back home."

Val looked at the empty seat beside her. "Shouldn't I ride in the back?"

"Is there a reason for you to?" she said.

Val decided not to answer that, and instead went to the passenger door.

He spent the majority of the ride with his forehead resting on his palm. The reality of Robin's death had not fully sunk in, let alone the horrible way it occurred. Then there was the shock from witnessing it, and the confusion surrounding the existence of a giant crab. On top of that, he felt helpless. There was a monster in the lake, and nobody believed him. Worse... they suspected *him* to be the killer.

Taylor let a few minutes pass before breaking the silence.

"You wanna tell me what happened."

A strained groan rumbled from Val's throat.

"I've explained it a hundred times."

"Val, I'm trying to help," she said. "I'm gonna be working late tonight to help with the search. It's obvious you didn't kidnap Ms. Berry and drag her to your house. I'm the one who found you unconscious on your floor. I saw the way the rug had tripped you. For you to run in like that, you had to have been scared out of your mind."

Val lifted his head. He was breathing through clenched teeth. He was thoroughly exhausted, yet full of nervous energy. His knees shook, his hands were constantly fiddling with each other, and he felt out of breath.

"What's there to tell. Robin's dead. Nothing I can say will bring her back."

"That's it?" Taylor said.

"What else do you want? I told you at the house, just like I told the detective five hundred freaking times. There's some animal in the water. It killed Robin, and unless you guys do something, it'll kill someone else."

Taylor nodded, her mind fixed on his use of the word 'animal'.

"You still sticking with giant crab?"

"I told the detective that it was dark, and that it was hard to see what it was exactly," Val said. "Maybe it was an escaped alligator that belongs to some zoo. I don't know."

Except he *did* know.

Val flinched, feeling the sensation of warm blood on his face and chest, his mind replaying the *thud* from Robin being rammed against the boat.

"Val? You okay?" Taylor said.

He put his left hand up to show her. "Yeah. I'm good."

"You don't look good."

"Christ, Deputy! I watched someone get torn apart right in front of me. That... that... that *thing* grabbed her. Cut her up with its claws! It was there! I saw it."

"A crab?"

"Fine! Let's call it a crab. That's what it looked like." He leaned against the headrest and relaxed himself. "You gonna report this conversation? Tell the detective that Valentine Krane is loony because he's talking about giant crabs in Lake Lucas?"

Taylor gave him a few extra seconds to calm down.

"No. Nothing you said here in incriminating. And Val..." She stopped at a stop sign and looked at him. "I'm not out to get you."

He nodded. It was his only way of saying 'thanks' right now.

"You still don't believe what I said about the crab, though."

Though it was a statement and not a question, Taylor answered it as such anyway. "Well, I'd rather go with the 'it was dark and something strange happened' explanation. Forgive me, but it's difficult to believe there are giant crabs in the water. And if there were, why hasn't anyone else seen them?"

"Probably because anyone who has is dead," Val said.

"We haven't had any homicide reports," Taylor said.

"It's a big lake, surrounded by thick woods. People who come to hike and camp around here generally prefer to be left alone. Not to mention the crappy cell service. If they wanted to call for help, they probably couldn't. At best, your department would get a call from a frantic family member informing you of someone who was overdue to come home."

He noticed the mild shudder in Taylor's expression. It was as if that statement had triggered a realization.

"Wait… you got a call from someone?"

Taylor felt foolish for letting her guard slip. "It may be nothing."

"*What* may be nothing?" Val said.

"We just got a call from some angry wife asking us to find her husband and nephew. I guess they came to the lake to fish, and haven't shown up yet." She looked at the clock on the radio. "I guess they were supposed to get back two hours ago."

"Are they answering their phones?"

"No, but like you said, cell service is spotty out here. Sometimes you get through, sometimes you don't."

The drive reached its conclusion at Val's driveway. He was relieved to see no cops were present, though caution tape had been placed around his dock and the shore, marking off his boats.

"They're letting me stay here?"

"They've set up a security camera," Taylor said. She pointed at a nearby tree. On the branch, a white camera was pointed at the dock. "Regardless of who caused it, your dock is officially the scene of a crime. They've spent the day inspecting your house, and found nothing. So yes, you're able to stay."

Val glared at the shore and the boats. That caution tape was another reminder of the suspicion the cops felt toward him. Beyond that dock was the lake. Its tranquility only served to unnerve him, for under that flat, glassy surface, a murderous fiend lurked.

His breathing intensified, drawing concern from the deputy.

"Val?"

"Don't go in the water," he said. "Just don't. There's something in that water. We need to alert everyone who has property on the lake, and set out a notice to all visitors. If we don't, it'll kill more people."

"Val. You need to calm down."

"Taylor, I'm not making this up," he said.

"Alright, shh," she said, reassuringly. "Listen, Alan and I are picking up the afternoon shift. We're going to be exploring around the lake. You just need to stay in your house and get your head straight. You're tired and edgy. Believe me, I know when someone's in need of a good night's sleep."

Despite the undercurrent of thinly suppressed panic, Val braved stepping out of the vehicle. He stood by the open door, watching the lake intensely. He was poised and ready to flee, feeling as though that thing would rise up at any moment.

The squeal of the radio made him jump several feet back.

Robin fumbled for the mic, caught off guard by her passenger's reaction.

"Yeah?"

"Hey, Davies? Where are you?" It was Alan Goldstein's voice.

"I'm on my way right now. Just had to help a friend with something real quick." She looked at Val. "Sorry man, I gotta go. Just get some rest, will ya?"

Val nodded, then shut her door.

"Thanks for the ride."

Taylor waved goodbye and backed out of the driveway, leaving him alone. All of a sudden, he felt terribly vulnerable. He did not own a firearm—he could not own one, due to being a felon. All he had was a baseball bat, some kitchen knives, and tools, none of which would be sufficient against that thing's shell.

After standing in the driveway, he slowly made his way to the house. The officers were at least courteous enough to clean up his living room. The cabinet doors and drawers had all been opened and thoroughly searched, however. His home resembled the aftermath of a major burglary. All of his closets were opened, the downstairs door opened, his over-the-counter drugs opened and searched in case they were hiding illicit substances.

Robin's things had been taken by the cops. It was just as well. Val had no desire to return them to her family members and open up the door to their chastisement. In all likelihood, they would blame him for what happened.

That thought sparked a new wave of hindsight.

Maybe they would be right to blame me.

Val sat on the living room chair. There was no way around it. he needed a drink to settle himself down. The first beer went bottom-up right off the bat, its contents guzzled. He tossed the empty bottle in the trash, then opened another.

He was already halfway through it when he sat in his living room chair, watching the lake with distrusting eyes. There was no mistaking what he saw last night. Robin was killed by a giant crab—a crab whose existence only *he* was aware of.

The rush of alcohol to his head sparked inspiration. He needed to do something to alleviate both the guilt and shock consuming him. Sitting here was only making things worse. Action was the only thing that would quell the turbulence in his soul.

I can't just sit here. Everyone needs to be warned. If I don't do anything, and those crabs kill anyone else, then it's on me.

Val quickly realized how he pluralized the crab. As far as he knew, there was only one. On the other hand, where there was one crab, there were usually others. It wasn't hard to assume the same rule applied to the giant ones.

He looked at the electric box laying near his sofa.

The wedding! They're setting themselves up for a buffet.

Val didn't hesitate to grab his truck keys and run out the door.

****

"Okay, just breathe. Slow down, it's alright... I know, I'm so sorry. I can't believe this has happened."

Barker and Dustin were unsure whether to be amused or disturbed by William Cook's convincing performance. The guy managed to perfectly mimic the cracking voice of a broken man, while rolling his eyes in boredom while he spoke to the grieving mother of Robin Berry. Unaware of their breakup, Ms. Berry called his cell phone after receiving word from the police of her daughter's death. The look on William's face made it clear he was not genuinely remorseful of Robin's sudden passing. If there was any sincere emotion, it was anger and jealousy, for Ms. Berry had confirmed Robin had gone to an ex-boyfriend's house.

"I know, it's crazy," he said, feigning sympathy. "She and I got in an argument. She saw that guy at the Arthur Bowen property, and just lost her mind... Yeah, that Valentine Krane guy, who robbed that bank and assaulted me after she *broke up* with him."

Barker snorted at that little twist of the narrative, drawing a fierce look from the drug addict.

"Yeah?... Did the police state his location?... Oh? They don't have enough evidence to arrest him? That's insane! Like, what else could possibly have gone down?... Alright, listen... I know, I know. Go to your sister's and stay with her... I'll try and speak with the cops and see what's going on... Okay, take care. Bye." He hung up. "Ugh! Finally! That old bitch sounded like her freaking tits were getting twisted while she blabbered on."

Barker and Dustin shared a brief glance, and a similar sentiment. *Well, she DID just learn that her daughter is dead...* Even degenerates like them understood basic human emotions.

"So, what now?" Barker said. "The cops think he did it, but haven't arrested him?"

"Looks like it," William said. He lit a cigarette and looked out the window. "That fucking bitch. I knew she was looking to fuck that guy. Whatever happened to her, it served her right."

"So, what's next?" Dustin asked. "We heading home?"

William took a few long draws on his cigarette.

"No."

"No?" Barker said.

"It's just as well the cops didn't arrest him," William said. "Now we have a better idea where the guy lives. Evidently, she was killed in a lake. That narrows down our search."

"It's a big lake," Barker said.

"Yeah, but for the most part, the lakefront residential properties are all on the northern end," William said. "I know what his truck looks like. We'll just drive around until we find him." He finished his cigarette and tossed it out the window. "Dustin. Give me the good stuff."

Reluctantly, Dustin passed him another bit of cocaine, which William happily snorted.

"Ahhhh..." He wiped his nose, then pointed west. "The hell are you waiting for? Let's go."

Barker suppressed a groan. Usually, he was more than happy to oblige his friend in kicking the shit out of someone. However, they had been here for almost a day, and he was eager to go home and meet with his usual whores. Good things would have to wait, unfortunately.

He started the engine and steered the vehicle out of the small parking lot, turning it west in the direction of Lake Lucas.

****

"What the hell are you doing here? Get out, or I swear I'll have you arrested!"

Val had not even stepped out of the vehicle before Arthur Bowen started verbally bombarding him. The lawyer marched into the driveway, followed by his wife and a few groomsmen. A few staff ascended up the hill, wearing mosquito spraying packs. One of them continued to spew white clouds of pesticide as he followed his boss to the driveway.

"For chrissake! Will you turn that stupid thing off!" the fat wife said, brushing the fumes away with her hand.

It wasn't long before the DJ with the stupid mustache and the bridesmaids were advancing up the hill.

To nobody's surprise, Leslie was instantly upset. She pointed a shaking finger at Val.

"What's *he* doing here?!"

"Listen…" Val stepped out of his truck and approached. "Please! I'm here to inform you—"

Two of the groomsmen grabbed him by the shoulders and held him back. One of them sniffed, then looked back at Arthur.

"I smell alcohol on his breath."

"Is that right?" Arthur said.

"No, no!" Val said. He stood up on his toes to see past the crowd. The wedding setup was almost complete. His memory served him right. It was right next to the shore. "Listen to me!"

"Nah, I don't think I will," Arthur said.

"You can't have the wedding tomorrow!" Val shouted.

"I've had enough." Arthur pointed at Dale and his groomsmen. "Get him out of here before I lose my temper."

"Please, wait!" Val said, holding up his hands. Two groomsmen, reeking of pesticide, pushed him back. "WAIT! You're in danger! There's something in the water! If you remain by the water, it may come after you!"

The whole crowd momentarily went silent, then broke out in laughter. Even Arthur cracked a grin.

"Guy really is drunk."

The only ones unamused were Leslie and Wanda. Leslie was tearing up.

"Why is he here?!" she said. "Why are you laughing? He's the one who killed Robin!"

Val's stomach felt as though a belt was compressing it. Obviously the news of Robin's death had reached this household. His jaw twitched as he searched for words.

"No. I didn't do it."

Arthur's smirk quickly vanished. Now, he had the look of a hardened lawyer who wanted to squeeze the opposition for all they were worth.

He looked to his wife. "Call the cops."

"Already on it," Wanda replied, dialing numbers into her cellphone.

"I'm serious!" Val said. "There's something in the water!"

"Sound like a crock of shit to me," Wanda said. "There's nothing in this lake other than a few bluegills."

"Yeah," Arthur said. "Tell us, Mr. Contractor, what exactly is in that lake that we should be so worried about?"

Val stood silent, at odds between the truth and the knowledge of how his answer would be perceived.

Arthur persisted, his presence increasingly intimidating.

"Well? Your tongue in a knot, Mr. Krane? Or did you not get your story straight before coming here?" Fed up, he looked to his wife. "Alright, I've had enough. Call the boys in blue."

"Crabs!" Val shouted.

For the second time, the group stood in stunned silence, then broke out into a fit of laughter. Just like before, Leslie and Wanda were the only ones not laughing.

"This man killed my friend and you're all laughing!" Leslie said.

"I didn't kill her," Val said. "Obviously you're not too broken up. Looks like you're going though as planned with the wedding."

That was the beer talking. Val shut his eyes and tightened his jaw.

Damn it. Why'd I say that.

The reaction was predictable. The groom, Dale Woods, strode at the electrician with intent to throw hands.

Arthur pulled the cigar from his lips, his eyes fiery with murderous anger. He may not have been enthusiastic about the wedding, but no way was he going to let someone insult his daughter's honor.

"Actually Wanda, *don't* call the cops."

Val read between the lines. All of a sudden, he realized exactly how bad of an idea coming here was.

He shook the groomsmen off of him and retreated to his truck. Luckily, the engine was still running. He put it in reverse and floored the accelerator. Once he was back on the road, he hightailed south for home.

He exhaled sharply. Coming here was a stupid idea, no matter how good his intentions. On top of that, he learned how unreliable his word had become. Nobody would believe his warnings about killer crabs in the lake. If the Bowen party knew the details of Robin's death, then likely the entire town was aware. Meaning the entire population suspected him to be a murderer. Anything he said from here on would sound like the ravings of a psychopath.

All he could do now was go home.

Home… the last place he wanted to be. Not only was it the place Robin was violently slaughtered, but he would be residing right by the lake—where that thing lurks. Anxiety took hold. He couldn't leave town. That would certainly get the police suspicious of him. Also, there was no chance he could get a motel in the area. Even if they weren't all booked with Arthur Bowen's guests, they would probably refuse service to him if he tried to check in.

First things first. Go home and figure this shit out.

He continued down the road, veering slightly to the right to avoid an oncoming rusty pickup truck that was hugging the middle.

****

"Well speak of the devil!" William Cook pointed his finger at the passing truck. "That's him! The son of a bitch!"

"You sure?" Barker asked.

"You saying I'm blind, dickhead?" William said. "I saw that truck yesterday. Turn around and fucking follow him, or I'll pull you out of the truck and beat your ass."

Barker gulped, then found a place to do a U-turn.

William shifted in his seat, barely able to contain his eagerness to get even with Val. He cracked his knuckles and licked his lips, imagining all the things he was gonna put the bastard through.

"I knew we were going too far north," he said.

"What's the plan? We gonna run him off the road?" Dustin asked.

"No," William said. "Just follow him. Let's see where he goes. With a little luck, he'll lead us right to his house. Then, when it gets dark, we'll pay him a special visit."

CHAPTER 16

"Show me the way to go home. I'm tired and I wanna go to bed. I had a little drink about an hour ago—"

"Jesus, Mary, and Joseph!" Taylor turned and looked at Officer Simon Heather. He cracked a smile while leaning against the side of their little patrol boat.

"What's the matter?" he said.

"Is that a serious question?" she said. "How 'bout the fact that I've had to listen to you sing the same tune fifty times. Geez, you make working with Alan enjoyable by comparison."

Alan looked up from the helm. "Hey! At least I was nice enough to get you a fresh cup of coffee."

"As long as you don't make me spill it," Taylor said.

"You've got nothing to worry about," Alan said. "We're on a boat. Not like I can hit the brakes."

Taylor eyed her coffee, which did not taste very good. Alan acted as though he bought it from the café or a Starbucks, when in fact he got it from a machine in the grocery store lobby. A machine which Taylor suspected hadn't been cleaned in a month.

Now that Simon was no longer singing, she could monitor the shoreline without wanting to stick an icepick through her eye. They had been patrolling the south part of the lake for a few hours now. The hardest part was checking all of the coves, which were heavily obscured by tree branches. So far, there was no sign of the missing persons.

They were nearing the now-vacant Ned Becker cabin. It had been three weeks, and still nobody knew what happened him. Last she heard, his family back in his hometown reported he was still missing. The office still got calls requesting for officers to search the woods and lake. After over two weeks of thorough searching, they found nothing. His vehicle was still parked in the driveway, the cabin's kitchen stocked with food and beverages, and the bedroom closet filled with clothes. There was no suicide note, or any other indication that he was about to take his own life—other than the fact that he disappeared right after his fiancée broke up with him.

Taylor was standing on the dock, standing by while the county dredged this part of the lake. No body was found. Ned's boat was still there, so they knew he didn't move to a different part of the lake. Nonstop searching of the surrounding woods did not produce any findings. The only oddity was some markings on the shoreline, as though a large branch had been dragged in the mud. Multiple rain showers diminished that so-called evidence. Everything else was completely normal. It was as though the guy simply disappeared.

"Looking at that place gives me the creeps," Simon said.

"Same," Alan said. He looked at the water. "It's safe to assume he didn't drown in the lake. Unless someone tied a ball and chain to him, his bloated corpse would've floated up at some point. Ugh, can you imagine if he is still down there somewhere? His meat would be all soupy, almost like Jell-O."

Taylor eyeballed her coffee, which now looked even less desirable.

"Thanks for that mental image," she said.

Alan turned the boat to the left and began crossing the lake to patrol the east side of it.

"Why'd you become a cop then, Taylor?" he said. "Expect to go through thirty years of this shit without seeing a rotted corpse?"

"When it's part of the job, I can accept it. Doesn't mean I enjoy thinking about it."

Simon chuckled obnoxiously. "You know who is enjoying it? The bluegills. They're probably thinking 'Ha! Stupid bastard. He ate a bunch of us, now we get to return the favor!'"

Taylor went ahead and dumped the coffee.

"You know, I'd call you a sick bastard, but you'd probably take it as a compliment."

Simon watched the little cloud of brown beverage disperse in the lake.

"*I'm* sick? You're the one polluting the lake."

"It's coffee!" Taylor said. "It's bio-degradable. Jesus, it's not like I threw my Styrofoam cup in the water. It's not like these fellas up there." She nodded to a stretch of shore to the north.

By the looks of it, someone had set up a camp. There was a folding chair on its side and a fishing pole laying on the shoreline. There was all kinds of debris in the grass, as though someone had spilled confetti all over the place.

"The hell kind of party happened up here?" Alan said.

"Don't know," Simon said. "Shall we take a look?"

"Might as well. Our so-called missing persons are nowhere to be found," Alan said. "Bugging these guys beats doing nothing at all."

Taylor rolled her eyes, instantly regretting bringing attention to the camp. As usual, Alan's superiority complex was showing its ugly face. He had no shame in his antics. A wannabe detective, he was always trying to find dirt on anyone he came across. Unless they had some kind of influence, such as Arthur Bowen. In that case, he became the ultimate kiss-ass.

He brought the boat near the shore.

All three officers felt the hairs on the back of their necks begin to rise.

"Wait a sec…" Alan brought the boat as close to shore as he could. "Is that…"

"Clothing," Taylor said.

"You sure?" Simon said.

"It's some kind of fabric," Taylor said.

"Hang on." Alan backed the boat up and gently brought it against the shore, killing the engine as soon as it touched the mud.

Taylor hopped off, hand resting on her sidearm. Alan was next to step off, while Simon opted to remain on the boat.

Immediately, they noticed how discolored the grass was. Something was coated over its natural green color. Equally as odd was the substance that had mixed with the mud. Whatever it was, it was brown in color.

Taylor knelt and picked up one of the pieces of fabric, then looked to her partner. "Flannel."

Alan picked up a different object, light brown in color with a black rubber piece attached to it.

"I think this is part of a boot." He walked further into the camp. The campfire was long burned out, with a kettle on top of it. There was a cooler full of beer and a cannister of coffee grounds. A tent was set up, undisturbed and vacant, a truck parked near the trees. Yet, there was no sign of the campers.

Taylor looked at the fishing rod on the shoreline. "You know many fishermen who leave their equipment laying around like this?"

"Nope. Even less who would leave a line unattended," Simon said, pointing at the taut line extending from the pole into the lake. He leaned down for a closer look at the line. Sure enough, it was twitching. "I think he's got a bite."

Alan did the honors. He picked up the rod and reeled in the line, bringing in a fourteen-inch bass. It dangled from the line, its mouth red and white where the hook was embedded. The fish, though alive, did not flounder. It appeared to be lethargic, having been stuck on the line for a significant amount of time.

His sense of humor was gone as he looked at the fish with a growing apprehension.

"I don't like this," he said.

Taylor walked to the truck and checked the driver's side door. It was unlocked. Nobody was inside. She opened the center console and found the registration.

"This truck belongs to a Timothy Henn," she said.

Alan went through the tent, popping back out with two wallets. He opened them up and found the IDs.

"Yep, Larry Henn and Timothy Henn." He looked at the coffee kettle, then peeled back the lid. "Looks like they were prepping some brew. Doesn't look like they got around to having their joe, though." He tossed the wallets back in the tent, then walked over to Taylor. "I *really* don't like this. We should call this in."

"Yeah, no shit. We should've called this in when we found the shredded clothes covered in down there."

"You sure that's blood?" he said.

"What else could it be?"

"Hard to tell in the mud." Alan sighed, accepting the likelihood she was right. "If it is blood, it's at least a day old. Maybe two. If there was a murder here, where the hell are the bodies?"

"You think one of the brothers went apeshit on the other?" Simon asked.

"If so, why leave the wallets for us to find?" Taylor said. "Why leave this camp intact at all?!"

Alan walked the length of the camp, studying its oddities, particularly the bits of clothing. Resigned, he clicked his radio transceiver.

"Dispatch?"

"Go ahead."

"Send a forensics unit to the southeast end of Lake Lucas. There's a camp here with signs of foul play. Deputy Heather will remain on scene. Deputies Davies and I will conduct a search on foot to attempt to find the missing parties. Just a heads up; we might have at least one deceased person in these woods."

"Copy that."

Alan looked at Taylor, then tilted his head toward the woods.

"Let's get started."

****

They first searched the section of woods nearest to the camp, finding no further clue as to what occurred at this camp. After five minutes, additional deputies arrived. After twenty minutes, forensics joined the scene. Photos were taken and samples were collected. Everyone came to the same conclusion: something dreadful had occurred on this campsite.

Alan and Taylor continued their search to the southern tip of the lake. Though in the woods, they made sure to keep the lake in view, believing that any clues would most likely be found near the shore.

Searching for a body in the woods carried a dreaded sense of anticipation. It wasn't clear what they would find exactly, especially after seeing the remains on the camp. Taylor braced herself for the possibility that she would see a mass of body parts, as though the victim had been through a chipper shredder. In addition, she was curious as to whether they were the only ones in these woods. She and the other deputies used to kid around about hunting an ax murderer in the woods. Now, that scenario seemed all too real.

Taylor lagged a few steps behind Alan, nervously watching her surroundings.

"You think this is odd?" Taylor said.

Alan stepped over some decaying branches, unsure whether to chuckle or sneer at that question.

"Nah. We find diced up people all the time!" he said. "Yes, of course it's odd. For people to just disappear like that? If their bodies were in the lake, they'd be topside by now."

"No, I mean… odd that this happened around the same time as the Robin Berry incident?" Taylor said.

Alan stopped and looked back at her. This time, he was chuckling.

"You're not buying this shit about killer crabs, are you?"

Taylor hesitated before answering. "No, of course not."

"Wow. I'm convinced. Word of advice? Keep that thought to yourself. It's not like this whole investigation hasn't gotten weird enough." He took a few more steps, then stopped abruptly. Immediately, he put his hand over his mouth and nose. "Apparently, I spoke too soon."

Taylor caught up with him, then gazed at the pool of flesh on the ground. Flies and mosquitos buzzed around it. Worms and roaches swam in the thick, coagulated puddles of blood.

Immediately, she was hit with a rotten smell which made the air feel like thick goo.

"Whoa!" she plugged her nose. "What is that?"

Alan slowly knelt by the assortment of brown fur, blood, and bone fragments. Using a stick, he prodded at the mass until he located a stiff, almost wooden object. He scooted it closer, revealing the hoof at the end.

"Just as I thought. It's a deer." He shrugged, noting the lack of a corpse. "*Was* a deer."

"A deer? Did it step on an IED?" Taylor waved a hand at the blood that had splattered on the surrounding trees and bushes.

Alan shook his head. "Looks more like something pinned it here and had its way with it."

"You say that like it's normal!"

"Well, there's been coyote sightings around here," Alan said. "Maybe the deer was injured and made for easy prey."

"That's a damn stretch," Taylor said.

"Yeah, but it technically adds up." He swallowed. "I hate to suggest it, but it's possible that's what happened at the camp."

"That's an even bigger damn stretch."

"Says the woman who's considering some criminal's story about giant crabs."

Taylor stood up and walked around the remains. "Maybe we should call this in."

"The team's at the camp. We'll let them know about it when we get back. I don't see a point in diverting personnel because we found a dead animal in the woods." He stood up and followed her to the south. "Let's keep looking."

As they walked away, Taylor gave one last glance at the remains. The ground was marked, as though several sticks or branches had been dragged through the dirt. There was no resisting the mental image of jagged crustacean legs, their pointed tips marking the earth while huge pincers tore at a helpless deer.

Really odd coincidence we find this after Val's testimony.

They crossed another few hundred feet of distance. By now, Alan was using his flashlight. There was still plenty of sunlight, but the canopy and thick vegetation made certain areas dark as night.

It took several minutes for the smell of rotted meat to escape Taylor's senses. Her heart was still pounding from the initial shock. Here they were, looking for a body, fearing to find it in the worst condition imaginable, and ultimately finding it. Just not the body they were looking for.

Alan continued taking the lead, now angling to the right to follow the bend of the shoreline. They had reached the southern end of Lake Lucas.

"Up ahead there's that creek," Alan said. "We haven't gotten much rain lately, so it should be fairly dry."

"We're a little far from the campsite, aren't we?" Taylor said.

"It's called a search, Taylor. We're branching out. If there's anything closer to the camp, the other deputies will find it."

He stopped and aimed his light up ahead.

"Creek's up there." He sniffed. "Something *else* is up there too."

Taylor could smell it as well. There was no mistaking the smell of rot.

Not again.

Even Alan was apprehensive. One dead animal, even as ravaged as that deer, wasn't too concerning. Multiple dead animals in a small area indicated a pattern.

He continued onward, keeping his right hand resting on his sidearm.

As they neared, the smell intensified. Already, it was far more rank than the deer remains. Once again, the smell created a sense of thickness in the air, as if Taylor and Alan were walking through a series of giant spiderwebs. This sense enhanced their already strong awareness of their surroundings.

Alan's hand was now tightly gripping his pistol, ready to unholster it at a moment's notice. Despite the lecture he gave a few moments ago, he was now questioning the decision to branch out this far. This section of woods felt haunted now. A childish apprehension came over him. His imagination ran wild, conjuring horrible images of figures waiting in the woods, hungry for slaughter, watching him.

"Alan?"

He looked at Taylor, then saw her finger pointing ahead to the right. He followed its direction with his eyes, then saw the patch of fur just beyond a grove of trees.

After a couple more steps, he could hear the buzzing of flies. Which was interesting, because the ground at his feet was completely covered with dead insects. Flies, mosquitos, may flies, bees, wasps—they were everywhere. As he glanced around, he noticed a few dead birds.

The only reasonable explanation was that somebody did some chemical spraying around here.

A lot of spraying.

The dead furry animal was a raccoon, laying on its side at the edge of the creek. Its front legs were coiled, its mouth slack, tongue protruding at a curved angle. A few meters past it, a few dead squirrels lay in various states of decay. Flies and other insects buzzed around, many of them dying and setting near the very corpses they intended to feed on.

The creek itself was fairly dry, as Alan predicted. There was a small stream at the bottom which fed into Lake Lucas.

Its center was lined with the corpses of more animals. Possums, raccoons, birds, even a few coyotes. None were immune to whatever plague had swept through this area.

The deputies stood at the edge of the creek, taking in the sight of mass death with increased apprehension.

"What's that?" Taylor said.

Alan looked at the rigid object in the middle of the array of death. From up here, it resembled a greyish, oddly shaped rock. Several yards behind it was another object of similar texture and color, but different in shape. This one closer resembled a piece of pipe, with one end jointed, the other one pointy.

"I don't know," Alan said.

"It looks like…"

"Don't fucking say it."

"A shell."

Alan hung his head, refusing to believe the absurdity. The exasperation lasted a moment, for a new realization grabbed his attention.

"Oh, no. This creek connects to Lake Alocasia, doesn't it?"

"It does," Taylor said. She put the pieces together in her head. "Oh, crap. They found nuclear waste dumped in the lake."

Alan snatched his speaker mic. "Dispatch, this is Sergeant Goldstein. We're going to need a hazmat team at the creek on the north side of the lake. And dispatch, tell them to bring a Geiger counter."

CHAPTER 17

By the time the third evening beer entered his system, Val's hands finally stopped shaking. Now, he felt dehydrated and woozy. It wasn't often someone could genuinely say that alcohol consumption helped them focus. Being in prison, Val knew his fair share of inmates who were incarcerated due to some sort of alcohol-related incident. Most of them denied their addiction and justified their excess use as 'fun'. The ones who were conscious of their problems usually were drinking or injecting to suppress memories. Sometimes it was crimes. Sometimes it was victimhood.

Val looked at the five beer bottles arranged on the edge of his computer desk. Two were from earlier that day, the other three consumed in rapid succession. It was all he could do for now. That, and search for evidence on the internet.

First, he looked up 'giant crabs' and was met with numerous science fiction results. *Island Claws; Attack of the Crab Monsters; Port Sinister; Mysterious Island; Space Probe Taurus.*

Then there were articles regarding somebody named Guy N. Smith.

"What the hell does this guy have to do with crabs?!"

He exited the window.

Frustrated from the search results, Val eyeballed his fridge. The remaining beer in there was calling his name. He stood up and walked to the fridge, nearly succumbing to temptation. Instead, he went for the coffee pot.

He put in the water and grounds, then leaned against the kitchen island while it brewed. While he waited, he drank half a bottle of water, then watched the world outside darken. The sunset took him right back to yesterday's horrible events.

Every time he closed his eyes, he saw those black, fuzzy claws grabbing at Robin. He was frequently wiping his face to get the sensation of warm blood off of him.

Don't think about it. Just watch the coffee.

Val focused on the black water drilling into the carafe. Maybe it was the beer in his system or the effort to not think about Robin. Regardless, he was mesmerized by the simple transformation of purified water into coffee. Such a simple process changed the very essence of the liquid. It was more than a change in color. It now contained a chemical stimulant which limited the reabsorption of sodium in cells, and increased flow of fluid to the kidneys. It was a completely different thing altogether.

Change...

Val felt his neurons fire.

"Those crabs obviously aren't normal. They've been changed. Altered. *Mutated*!"

He returned to the computer and tapped the keyboard with his fingertips. 'Wildlife mutations.'

The first images on screen were animals that lived near Chernobyl. Each one was more grotesque than the last. There were pigs with two noses, deformed deer, cows with extended jaws, wolves with legs too small—or too long. Some creatures grew far larger than nature intended due to the radiation that had infested that area.

"Radiation... Holy shit!"

He typed 'Lake Alocasia environmental disaster' in the search bar. Numerous articles appeared on the screen, most of which spoke of the efforts to clean out the lake and destroy the infected wildlife.

He backspaced, then typed a new search. 'Mutations in Lake Alocasia.'

The first images were of baby bluegills with bulging eyes, protruding scales, and overgrown dorsal spines. At first, they appeared to be normal sized. Then Val read the text, which stated that scientists had confirmed several of these fish were only a few days old.

The more he scrolled, the more genetic mutations were shown. There were worms twice as long as they were before. Pregnant deer that were exposed to the radioactive water had given birth to horrible deformities. It was unclear how long the radioactive waste had been in that lake, but judging by these effects, it had to have been a couple of years.

Val continued scrolling, seeing nothing about crab sightings. It could not be a coincidence. That crab that killed Robin must have been exposed to the nuclear waste.

A simple question came to mind. Crabs were usually found on the coast, but this was northern Mississippi. Did crabs live inland?

'Freshwater crabs in U.S.A.'

The results made Val's stomach tighten.

The Chinese mitten crab, an invasive species from Asia, had been reported on the East Coast as well as San Francisco, and the Gulf of Mexico. They can live in both freshwater and saltwater. They are named for claws which are covered in patches of dark setae, which resemble fur. In Asia, they dwell in rivers, estuaries, and lakes. They tend to burrow, and have been found in depths of ten meters.

Val didn't need the text to know that ugly crustacean was the culprit. He looked at its long spider-like legs, the fuzzy white-tipped claws, the black color.

'Chinese mitten crab in Lake Alocasia.'

Sure enough, he found articles about the invasive species. According to the reports, it was believed they migrated up the Mississippi River, then traveled to nearby lakes and ponds. Two years ago, the Department of Wildlife issued a public service announcement informing people to kill the crustaceans if found.

"Apparently, they didn't get that memo soon enough," Val said. He rested his head in his hands as he absorbed the facts of the matter. The crabs were in Lake Alocasia, got mutated by the radioactive waste, likely remained burrowed in the deeper regions, which prevented them from being found. They hunted at night, gorging themselves on mutated fish, deer that came to shore for a drink...

"And the Shenkarow family."

He recalled a snippet he caught on the radio yesterday morning.

"Efforts to clean up the disaster are now resuming after the strange disappearance of the Shenkarow family, who mysteriously disappeared while camping near one of the coves."

Then there was the disappearance of that fella on the south end of Lake Lucas.

"The creek. They migrated through the creek into Lake Lucas."

A knock on the door made him jump.

"Hello? Anyone home?!"

Val stood up, then peeked out his window at his driveway. There was a truck parked beside his. It was tough to see its features in the dark. From what he could tell, he didn't recognize it.

The visitor knocked again. "Hello? Sorry to bother you. I blew a tire and I don't have a spare. I don't have a phone. I really could use some help."

Val stood up, hesitant to answer the door. What were the odds someone would show up out of the blue on the same day the whole town suspected he was a murderer.

"Sorry, I can't help you," he replied.

"Sir, please. I really need help. I'm traveling through town and I don't know anyone in the area."

"You have a spare?"

"No, regrettably."

Val clenched his teeth. His gut was warning him against answering the door, but the decent human within was chastising him for not helping someone in need. He didn't recognize the person's voice, so it seemed reasonable that the guy simply came to the first property he saw after rupturing his tire.

You're probably looking too far into this, Val.

"Hang on." Val went to the door. He unlocked it and opened it. The man turned around, his face and neck covered in tattoos.

Nope! You were right on the money!

That realization came too late. Two other men appeared from around the corner, one a tall, slightly out of shape man, the other William Cook.

The latter was the first to strike. Val was struck across the chin, causing him to stumble back into the house. William pressed the attack, tackling Val to the floor. The other two attempted to join in, but in their clumsiness, got jammed in the doorway when trying to enter at the same time.

"Come on, you dumb fucks!" William shouted.

Val shoved his palm against William's nose, momentarily jamming his airway and weakening his grasp. Val repeatedly hammered his fist into William's face. There was no technique to his method. Just a primal drumming of fists until the drug-crazed attacker was off of him.

On his feet, Val retreated into the kitchen. The other two were running after him with remarkable enthusiasm. They split apart, the larger one running over the furniture to flank him. In that moment, the tattooed one sprang. For a scrawny fella, he was surprisingly strong. He drove Val against the computer table, pinning him there.

His attack didn't last long. Val grabbed one of his empty beer bottles and cracked it over the guy's head. The skinny tattooed man fell on the floor, clutching his brow with both hands while moaning.

The bigger one was a couple steps away. Val knew there was no winning this matchup. The guy was too big and crazed. He raised the bottle, which was still intact after being used as a club, and chucked it. The big guy raised his arms over his face, deflecting the bottle into the hallway.

It stalled him enough for Val to make a run to the kitchen. There was a back door he could escape through.

That plan would never come to pass. The big guy managed to close the gap and grab Val by the shirt. The two men stumbled in a circle while the victim tried to escape. Increasingly angry, the big guy adjusted his grip, spinning Val to face him.

His knee came up into Val's groin, doubling him over and ridding him of strength. A haymaker dazed him more than the five beers combined. The abuse continued, with Val's head being slammed against the countertop.

William and the tattooed guy ran into the kitchen. A series of punches followed, battering Val until he was sprawled out on the floor.

William bookmarked the assault with a kick to the groin. Val could barely breathe. Two shots to that region would get the best of any man.

He rolled to the fetal position, gasping for breath.

The three men stood over him, the two associates looking to William to direct the next course of action.

"Yeah. A big buy named Barker... don't ask... and a skinny drug addict dipshit named Dustin. You'd see him a mile away thanks to his tattoos."

Robin was right. William called his equally degenerate buddies, and instead of going back home, they decided to track him down.

"Get out of here," he said. He knew saying that was as useless as a pen without ink.

The three men laughed.

"Oh, sure. I guess we'll go!" William said. He stomped on Val's stomach for good measure. His smile was gone. In its place was a monstrous sneer revealing crooked, decaying teeth. "Listen, you fuck. You think you got the better of me? First you fucked Robin, then you killed her!"

"I didn't kill her. Not like you care," Val groaned.

William's hideous grin reappeared.

"Well, there may be some truth to that. I do appreciate you not denying the fact that you fucked her." He nodded to Barker, who grabbed Val and lifted him to his feet.

A blow to the gut put Val on his knees. Barker began to lift him again, but was stopped by William.

"No, no, no. Keep him right there. That's perfect." That grin widened as William began to undo his fly. "It's time you learn, Krane. You're my bitch."

Dustin stepped away with one eyebrow raised.

"Uh… I thought you said we weren't going to…"

"Shut up!" William revealed his enlarged manhood to Val, then pointed at it. "Suck it! Then *maybe* we won't break every bone in your body."

Val clenched his jaw. Contrary to what many of his peers thought, he never had to endure this in prison. His throat tightened and his mind raced. He shifted, relearning quickly that he would not outmuscle Barker.

William thrust his hips toward his face. "Put it in your mouth! Do it now. Open wide."

"Do it," Barker said, pushing Val toward it. "You can do it with your teeth in, or out. Your choice."

William chuckled. "Don't worry. We'll let you have a drink to wash it down after."

A drink.

Val looked to the countertop, and the freshly brewed pot of coffee atop of it. With all of his might, he shifted his body weight toward the counter. Just a few inches was all he needed.

His fingers grasped the handle, yanked the pot off the drip pan, and splashed the boiling-hot contents onto William's anatomy. The drug addicted woman abuser let out a high-pitched scream that sounded like something from deep in the Amazon Rainforest.

Val swung the pot backwards over his head, crashing it against Barker's face. The brute yelped and lost his grip, allowing Val to stand up. He had a split-second to choose his escape route. Barker, though his face was bleeding, still stood between him and the back door. Dustin was near the kitchen table, a moment away from lunging at him. William was on his back, clinging to his smoldering manhood. Beyond him was the front door.

Val hopped over the writhing criminal and went for the front door, scooping his smartphone up as he passed the computer desk.

"GET HIM!" William shouted, his voice having a squeaky quality to it.

Val went out the front door and turned the corner, hoping to get to his truck. Barker was already outside, having gone out the back entrance to intercept.

"Shit." Val backed up, seeing Dustin stepping out the front door. The adrenaline had worn off, the pain in his own groin returning. Hunched forward slightly, he backed toward the lake.

Barker and Dustin advanced, then stopped momentarily as William stumbled through the front door. He was doubled over, his quivering hands working to secure his pants.

"Get him, you idiots!"

Val backed up, with nowhere to go except the dock.

"Get away!" he said. The two thugs kept coming. Val increased his pace to the best of his ability, quickly arriving at the shoreline.

Barker and Dustin sprang. Val threw a haymaker, catching Dustin on the nose. He then threw a left, hitting Barker in the ribs. It didn't stop the big bastard, who retaliated with a right cross of his own. Val, still aching from the last beating, went down easily. Once again, he was bombarded with a few kicks. The phone bounced from his grasp, landing a few feet out of reach.

William hobbled to the lake, breathing heavily. He picked up Val's dropped phone and chucked it in the lake.

"Thought you were gonna call for help, huh?" William tried to smile, but groaned in pain. After resting for a moment, he looked to Barker. "Get him back on his knees."

"Wait…" Dustin said. "You're not seriously going to make him… you know. Especially not after—"

"Shut up, moron. No, I can't. That's why *you're* going to make him do it instead."

Dustin's face flushed.

"Dude, I'm willing to beat him to death right here and now. But *that*… I'm not into that."

"Shut up and do it!" William said. "I want this bastard's last moments to be as miserable as possible."

Panic struck Val, and he tried to wrestle away. Barker stumbled backward, struggling to keep his victim under control. They stumbled several steps into the water until he was able to wrestle Val back to his knees.

"Hurry up, Dustin," he said.

"I mean…"

"Just picture Anna Lorell. She looked like a dude anyway."

"Hang on…" Dustin pulled out his baggie of cocaine and took a big snort. He leaned his head back and shut his eyes. "Oh, that's better. Mmm… Anna Lorell. How I miss that taste."

Val's stomach tightened as he watched Dustin relax a bit. The drugs erased any apprehension.

Dustin pointed to the shoreline. "You mind bringing him over…"

"No. If I loosen up, he may try to run again. Just come in the water. Hurry up so William doesn't get pissed."

"Allllllright." Dustin waded into the lake, undoing his pants.

Val felt the urge to regurgitate. He was so close to escaping this predicament, only to end up having to choke down an even uglier dude's piece. His strength was almost entirely depleted. Outmuscling Barker was impossible.

Dustin dropped his pants. "Alright, Anna Lorell. Do what you do best."

Val shook. "Fuck you, you fucking…"

Dustin backhanded him across the face. "Now, you do what you're told, little missy!" He extended it towards Val's tightly shut lips. "Come on, now. Not too rough. If I feel any edges, I swear I'll—"

The water erupted. Dustin reared back and screamed as rigid edges clamped down on his manhood.

"HOLY SHIT!" Barker released his grip and retreated from the humongous black crab which spawned from the lake.

Its right claw was shut tight, holding Dustin in place. The tattooed druggie waved his arms and hollered at the top of his lungs.

Val fell to his side, then crawled on his hands and knees toward shore. When he found land, he looked back, just in time to see the crab attempt to pull its victim closer. The 'appendage' snapped off with ease, the fleshy stump spurting blood.

Dustin stood in shock, looking down and screaming at the big red spot where his dick had been.

The crab, dissatisfied with the dinky amount of flesh, lunged at him. It drove him on his back, then began cutting away at his torso. In a few seconds, his midsection was opened up, his innards exposed and lit by the dock light.

As it fed, a second crab emerged from the water. It ignored the injured human and scurried toward the fresh meat directly ahead of it.

It was exactly like what Val saw on the computer screen, only more grotesque. Its mandibles resembled bony spider legs, dripping fluid. Its legs were long and somewhat thin relative to its size. Had it not been for the claws, he could've easily mistaken it for a spider.

Once again, Val had to make a split-second decision. Go for the truck, or hide in the house. He decided to go for the house.

It proved to be the right choice. The crab darted forward, ignoring him for the time being in favor of Barker. At that moment, the brute learned he had something in common with the crab: they both moved amazingly fast for their size.

Barker almost reached his rusty truck.

Almost.

"No! NO! NOOOO!"

It's pincers closed over his hamstring, cutting through flesh and muscle. The pain induced made wrestling Barker to the ground easy. He was facedown, flailing his arms about. The crab stepped over him, its claws panning back and forth, searching for a new area to grab.

It chose both of his upper arms, shutting tight enough to snap the bones. Barker squealed, then squealed again as the thing lifted him up. He was on his knees, held up by his attacker—while a third crab emerged from the lake and scurried toward him.

"Oh God! Oh shit! Oh Christ!" His attempts to escape were worthless, for his attacker was stronger than he was. It held him in place, its mandibles attempting to open the back of his head.

The third one closed the distance, doubling its speed in the last few yards. Its upper claw plunged through Barker's gaping mouth, piercing the back of his throat. The pincer shut, slicing his cheek and jaw muscle. He lashed again, parting Barker's lower jaw from his head.

He remained on his knees, tongue flapping freely, blood gushing from where his chin used to be.

The crab fed on the bony lump of flesh, then grabbed Barker by the neck. The other crab, eager to keep its prize, tugged Barker's arms. The two crabs tugged back and forth, their prey groaning in agony.

The meat on his upper arms began to stretch like gel. The pincers holding them tightened their grip.

Split.

Barker fell forward, spurting blood from the two stubs where his biceps used to be.

The victorious crab pulled him by the neck away from its opponent, who was busy feasting on one of the arms. Content that it would not have to compete further for this meal, it decided to feed. Barker squirmed as the pincers tightened around his neck, slicing flesh and arteries. Before his brain could shut down from blood loss, he got to endure the unbearable pain of his neck bone snapping.

Val could see the carnage in his peripheral vision as he hobbled though his doorway. Barker's body, headless and armless, twitched while his slayer picked away at his torso.

He stepped inside, locking the door behind him.

A moment later, he heard running footsteps approaching. The outside knob shifted, the door tremoring from the efforts of a panicked William Cook.

"LET ME IN! LET ME IN!"

Val didn't have a chance to choose between his better nature and his bitter resentment.

The crab that devoured Barker's arms turned around, drawn by William's cries. It raised its pincers and darted in his direction.

William shrieked then sprinted away from the door. In an effort that was nearly comical, the creature chased the drug addict literally in circles. Around and around they went, completing at least three laps in the front yard before William had enough sense to run for his pickup truck.

Huffing and puffing, he zipped for the rusty vehicle, gleefully slamming the door shut behind him. The respite he felt was immediately stripped away. He looked at the empty ignition, then at Barker's bloodied corpse. *He* had the keys.

"Oh, shit. SHIT!"

The crab arrived at his door. Its claws scratched the vehicle, grooving the door and wheel well. With incredible strength, it managed to rock the truck back and forth.

The chaotic sound attracted the other two, who abandoned their meals to attack what they initially thought was a large animal. Upon arriving, they realized the truck was not living or edible, but did contain something that was.

One mounted the engine, the other climbed into the bed. Together, they peeled away at the cab, racing for the fresh meat inside.

The crab on the engine proved to be the winner of this contest. William floundered in his seat, sprinkled with a barrage of broken windshield glass before two fuzzy claws pulled him out into the open. Scampering backward, it dragged William onto the lawn, then plunged its claws into his midsection.

William gagged and vomited blood, feeling his lower stomach, kidneys, and liver split open. The crab continued digging in, snapping some lower ribs and chipping his spine.

Its brethren darted after it, determined to steal the human away. One of them grabbed William by the leg, starting a second tug-of-war match. The defending crab seized William by the shoulders and pulled.

Blood drizzled from William's mouth as he tried to scream. His words came out half gargle, half croak.

"Hel—helllll—helllppp meeeee…"

The third crab joined in, grabbing him by the other leg. The defending crab concentrated its efforts on his right shoulder.

All three tugged with every ounce of energy.

SPLIT!

Like a criminal in medieval times, William was drawn and quartered. One of the crabs stepped aside, holding a leg in its claws. It turned away, content with feasting on the appendage… until it saw another figure peering through a glass square in the big habitat.

"Oh… oh…"

Val stepped away from the kitchen window, having witnessed the execution outside. His head was starting to spin. Stress and pain overloaded his brain.

He heard rapid thumping from huge legs approaching the house. Val looked to the window, then fell back as a huge claw punched through the glass. Like a moray eel reaching from its cave, it waved left and right, snapping its pincer like a serpent's jaw.

Val scooted backward on his hands and feet, making his way around the island. Consumed by terror, he stood up and sprinted for the basement door. He pushed it open, took a step… and tumbled down the steps, having tripped on the beer bottle he previously chucked at Barker.

For the second night in a row, he was knocked unconscious.

CHAPTER 18

Taylor Davies yawned, then glanced at her phone. She could not believe it was already a quarter after midnight. When she agreed to pick up overtime, she was under the impression she would be going home at nine at the latest. Now, she had worked her way into the midnight shift.

The creek was full of hazmat personnel, dressed in full body protective gear. Several third-shift deputies secured the area from afar, after marking off the area with caution tape. Already, the entire creek was cordoned from the public, due to the confirmation of dangerous radiation levels.

Simon and Alan stood beside her, their patrol boat docked at the Ned Becker cabin. Initially, they were both astounded at being part of what could be a high-profile investigation, especially Alan. That enthusiasm dwindled into complete sleep-inducing boredom as the hours dragged on. For a few hours, they continued the search for the missing campers, with no results. When it became too dark to comb through the woods, they returned to the creek area.

"We should have considered sealing off this creek when the spill was first discovered," Taylor said.

"They tested it repeatedly," Alan said. "The contaminated area was on the southern part of Lake Alocasia. The lake water doesn't really connect through the creek. It's mainly rainwater that fills this thing."

"It still makes for a bridge," Taylor said. She looked at her coffee... her seventh for the entire day. Drowsiness had made her cranky. That and, though she refused to admit it, the thought of Val with that Robin woman. She immediately felt stupid for feeling jealous. She and Val had no relationship. Above all, it was stupid for her to be jealous of a dead person, of all people. On that note, she knew better to keep her crush to herself. A cop having feelings for someone involved in a murder investigation was not a good look.

It was bad enough she was starting to buy into Val's story about crabs.

"Maybe we should head back," she said.

Simon made an obnoxious, childlike yawn. "Yeah, I'm on board with that. I'm beat."

"Maybe we can hitch a ride from one of the midnight shift deputies," Alan said. "Just leave the boat where it is. There'll be a crew here in the morning. Otherwise, we'll have to boat four miles up the lake to get to the SUV and trailer. Not like anyone's gonna steal it."

"Yeah… except I left my wallet in there," Simon said.

"How the hell did you forget your wallet?" Alan said.

"I didn't forget it," Simon replied. "I left it in the center console."

"Why?"

"Because I hate having that thing in my pocket all the time."

"That's what happens when you have a dozen credit cards," Taylor said. She turned to walk to the Becker property. "The sooner we get there, the sooner we can go home. Don't know about you, but I still have to be in by seven tomorrow."

"Unless you call in sick," Simon said.

"No. I'm not you," she replied.

The three of them waved goodnight to their midnight companions before heading over to the Becker property.

****

The ride back was nearly successful in lulling Taylor to sleep. Alan was too tired to initiate some kind of obnoxious banter. Simon did not assault her senses with his horrible singing voice. There was only the revving of the boat's motor, and the lakeside choir consisting of frogs, crickets, and the occasional loon.

Simon kept the spotlight on. The last thing he wanted was to sneak up on some night-owl fishermen. He panned the light across the water, occasionally pointing it at the shore.

"You looking for campers?" Alan said.

"No, I'm keeping an eye on the landscape so I know where we're going," Simon said. "It's dark and we're in the middle of a huge lake. It's not like there's street signs."

"Yeah? Your plan is to look at the shore and hope we don't pass the public dock?" Alan said.

"Dude, you must be really tired and bored if you're critiquing my navigation skills."

Taylor stared at the bright moon, begging for it to smash into the earth and spare her from listening to this conversation.

So much for no obnoxious banter.

"You guys really need to get a life," she said.

"Hey, point the finger at him," Simon said. "I was just standing here minding my own business." He redirected the spotlight into the water.

Alan stood up. "Hang on a sec. Point that back at the trees."

"Yeah? Why? Thought you saw a bear?" Simon said.

"No! Stop the boat and point the light where you had it."

Simon realized Alan was not playing around. He killed the engine then turned the spotlight to the right. The white stream grazed the shoreline, finding nothing but a thick grove of trees.

"What'd you see?" he asked.

"I don't know. I think it was a little further back."

"*What* was a little further back?"

"I don't know!"

Now Taylor was trying to look. "Alan, this better not be a game."

"Yeah, because I absolutely love fucking around after midnight after investigating *two* murder scenes." He watched Simon pan the spotlight down the line of trees. "There! Hold it right there."

There was something on the ground between two of the trees. Whatever it was, it was yellow in color and soft.

"That a shirt?" Taylor said.

"I don't think so. I see another one a couple feet away," Simon said, aiming the light slightly to the left. He dug a pair of binoculars out of the storage bin and aimed them at the lit area. "There's another one further back."

He passed the glasses to Taylor, who quickly took a look. All of a sudden, she was wide awake again.

"This remind you of anything?" Simon said.

"Yeah. Whatever it is, it's torn. Just like the clothing we found at that camp."

"Oh, you've got to be kidding me," Alan said. "I can't see if there's a camp right there. There's too many trees in the way."

"Hang on. There's a spot on the side where we can line up the boat," Simon said. He started the engine back up and pointed it towards shore. A few yards to the south was a fallen tree extending into the lake which served as a place to dock. After the boat was lined up, Alan and Taylor stepped out and secured the mooring lines to a branch.

The three of them cautiously stepped ashore, each one keeping a hand close to their sidearm. Already, there was a smell of rot, something which was getting too familiar now.

After passing through a thick collection of trees, they came across a clearing.

Taylor nearly dropped her flashlight. She stepped back, now checking the surrounding forest with her personal flashlight. After multiple sweeps, she pointed her torch back at the ravaged yellow tent, and the fly-covered pools of dried blood.

Right away, she clicked her radio transmitter. "Dispatch?" Nothing. "Dispatch?... Damn it! It's these stupid trees."

"More like these old radios," Alan said. "Mine needs to go back on the charger."

"Fact is, we need to get someone out here," Simon said. "I don't know about you, but this is the third murder site we've come across today. This isn't normal, guys!"

Taylor went to the tent, steering clear of the flies and blood. She got close enough to the tent to see the packed bags and the belongings. They were open, but were still fairly packed. Everything here resembled a standard camp setup.

"It's just like the other one. Nothing's stolen. It's just..." she pointed the light at the nearest blood puddle, and the bits of bone and hair mixed in. "Let's get out of here."

"I second that," Simon said.

They quickly returned to the patrol boat. Simon was the first to step aboard.

"Where's this place at?" he asked, holding the boat's mic. "Hard to get a team here if I can't give them an exact location."

"I think we're close to Valentine Krane's house," Taylor said.

"Good. We already have a good marker right here. Let's head up shore and see how far his place is from here."

Simon started the engine back up, eagerly putting distance between himself and the campsite. His fingers shook against the helm, the gravity of the situation weighing on him.

"What the hell is going on around here, guys?"

"I don't know," Taylor said. She watched the shore pass by. After speeding a little more than a half mile, she spotted a white dock light up ahead. "There! I think that's his place."

"Good." Simon neared the Krane property and slowed his boat. "How far is the camp from here? Two-thirds of a mile south?"

Taylor and Alan didn't answer, their attention fixated on the dimly lit driveway. They could see there were two trucks instead of one. Taylor moved to the spotlight and aimed it at the smaller truck.

"Whoa," Simon muttered. "You spying on the guy? He's allowed to have visitors... Oh..." His jaw dropped at the sight of the scrap heap that the two vehicles had been reduced to.

The larger one was unmistakably Val's. *Almost* unmistakably. The front tires were torn to shreds, the hood appearing as though a massive can opener had been taken to it. The second vehicle was far worse. The windshield was gone, tires shredded, driver's side door practically peeled apart, the cab overhead caved in.

The night had officially gotten weirder.

Simon moved the light onto the grass in front of the smaller truck. Pieces of clothing and footwear were scattered about, the grass noticeably darker even from their distance.

Simon grabbed the speaker mic. "Dispatch?"

"This is Dispatch. Go ahead."

"Dispatch, we need..."

THUMP!

All three cops looked down, feeling the vibration under their feet. Taylor and Alan looked to each other.

Alan pointed down. "Did something just..."

The lake came alive on the bow of the boat. Two enormous eels rose from the water, their skulls fuzzy, their snouts narrow and pointed. They grabbed the edge of the boat and began to pull.

"Holy shit!" Simon jumped back, dropping the radio.

As the cops bunched on the main deck, a second pair of 'serpents' rose from the water. They snapped at the air before plunging into the hull of the boat, less than a foot from Taylor's hip.

She gasped, seeing the bony jaws clamp onto the boat.

The boat leaned, causing her partners to fall against her.

Alan drew his pistol and fired off several rounds point blank at one of the creatures. The bullets skidded off a rigid shell.

In the water, behind the 'necks' of these two creatures, a disk-shaped object began to emerge. Eight digits, like rigid tentacles, protruded from its sides. Two eyes, mounted on stalks, gazed at the frightened officers.

At that moment, they realized that these 'eels' biting at their boat were indeed crab claws.

There were two of them, working in unison to drag the boat into the water.

Simon was the first to descend into panic. "Mary, Jesus! They're giant fucking crabs! Holy God!"

"They're turning the boat over!" Alan shouted.

In the span of an instant, four thoughts flickered through Taylor's mind. *We just discovered the answer to the many disappearances around Lake Lucas; Oh God, Val was telling the truth; We need to get to shore now; HOLY SHIT, WE'RE BEING ATTACKED BY A GODDAMN CRAB!!!!*

She focused on the third one.

"Jump! Swim to shore! Hurry up!"

She climbed over the starboard gunwale, then nosedived into the lake. Alan fired his remaining rounds at the crab, then followed her, gripping his Glock tight as he swam for shore.

Simon hesitated, the prospect of going into the water seeming like suicide. Then again, staying here was certainly suicide. Water spilled over the gunwale, the portside now completely in the water.

With no other choice, Simon climbed over the seats and over the starboard side of the boat.

Splash!

Taylor was the first to reach the shore. Her wet uniform was three times as heavy now. Her radio and phone were soaked.

"Dispatch? Hello?" The lack of response confirmed her fear. This wasn't a signal or battery issue. The radio was dead.

Alan scampered on all fours, frantic and confused. He ejected his empty mag and tugged at the pouch strap to extract a spare.

"Giant crabs, my God! I can't believe Val was telling the truth," he said.

Taylor now had her weapon drawn. She kept it low, watching as Simon neared the shoreline.

Several yards behind him, the boat was beginning its descent into the lake. One of the crustaceans was mounted on its bow, probably in hopes of finding any lingering prey. After a few short moments, it turned around, pointing its big black eyes at the group.

Splash.

"Oh Jesus… Simon, hurry up! It's coming!"

"I'm coming! I'm coming!" He reached the shallows and was not striding toward land. "Don't let it get—" He fell forward, splashing face first into the water.

Cursing under his breath, Alan ran to his aid. He grabbed Simon by the shirt and pulled him up.

"You clumsy idiot."

"Get me out!" Simon said. "My foot's caught on something!"

Alan pulled him onto the shore, dragging the object behind him. As it emerged out of the water and into the dock light, they took in the sight of the bloated eyes, sagged meat, and exposed ribcage of a human corpse.

Simon screamed, realizing his foot was snagged in the dead man's stomach. Curved ribs poked at his calf and shin, the inside squishy and solid all at once.

"Get it off! Get it off!" He tried to shake his foot loose, but the organic trap managed to cling tight. The head rolled in his direction, peering at him with wet white eyes. The skin on the face and neck was discolored, both by tattoo ink and loss of blood.

With his gaze locked on the horrific view, Simon was blind to the large swell of water rolling in his direction—until it was too late.

"Look out!" Taylor shouted.

The water parted, making way for the big black crab. It rose on its eight legs, its claws extending from its carapace. The big pincers repeatedly snapped, taunting their prey.

Taylor squeezed the trigger. The round struck the crab in the side, breaking apart against the rigid shell. The crab took no notice of the impact. Several more shots followed, each one as useless as the last.

It advanced on Simon, who was now lost in a storm of panic. He squirmed in the mud, struggling to remove his gun from its holster. Alan tried dragging him further up the shore, but could not outpace the beast. In the blink of an eye, it was standing on top of Simon.

Huge pincers snapped at Alan, who had no choice but to let go of his partner and jump out of reach.

"No! No! No! Don't let it get me—AHH!"

It got him.

Blood jetted from Simon's trunk. Huge slabs of meat peeled off his body like the husk from an orange. Even as his insides were fully exposed, Simon still tried to crawl away.

Taylor and Alan both shot at the crab, which seemingly took no notice while it began to devour Simon alive.

The arrival of a second crab forced them to redirect their aim. The crab darted up the shore, followed by a third. The bombardment of nine-millimeter rounds stopped them momentarily. The crabs flourished their mandibles, unhurt but rather confused by the bizarre stings.

Taylor looked at the locked slide of her weapon, then at the crabs. They were on the move again, claws cocked and ready to lash. She loaded a fresh magazine and backpedaled, now screaming as she squeezed off shots.

****

At first, Val thought he was awakening to the sound of fireworks. When he lifted his head, he realized he was on his basement floor. His head, shoulders, and legs were throbbing, thanks to hitting a dozen steps on the way down.

He wasn't sure how long he was out. Probably a few hours. Had it not been for the repeated bursts of noise, he likely would have drifted off again.

Bang! Bang! Bang! Bang!

Even to his groggy mind, it was quickly evident what he was listening to. Gunshots, loud and near. And screams. A female voice.

Taylor Davies.

He sprang to his feet and ran up the stairs, through the house, to the front door. The locked handle was cranking repeatedly.

"Shit! Shit!" A fist pounded on the door. "Val! You in there?! Let us in!"

Val opened the door and was immediately pushed aside by a frantic Alan Goldstein.

Outside, Taylor was shooting her pistol at two crabs. The third was near the lake, holding the severed arm of a limp corpse in its claws.

"Taylor! Get in!"

She turned to the sound of his voice, then sprinted for the door. Val slammed it shut as soon as she was inside.

Immediately, it splintered. Two ends of a pincer pierced the door, nearly impaling Val. He jumped back, amazed at the ease in which the crustacean tore at the door.

Before, they had not bothered pursuing, probably due to being distracted with their other kills. Now, the only available meat was in this house.

The crab reduced the door to a pile of plywood, then tore at the frame.

"It's getting in!" Taylor said.

"Yeah, I can see that!" Val said. It was clear the thing would be inside in a few seconds. The house was no longer a sanctuary. Their best shot of survival was getting the hell out of here. "Out the back door. Let me get my truck keys... oh shit..."

"What?"

Val grimaced, remembering that the crabs had torn up his truck. "Yeah... I doubt my truck'll work."

He looked to the doorway in time to see the crab begin prying its way through.

"Where do we go?" Taylor said.

"The neighbor's house," Val said. "I have the key. Hurry! Out the back way." He grabbed his keys they led them to the back door. He stepped out, turned the corner, then held his hands out. "STOP!"

Alan had stepped outside behind him, then quickly ducked back inside. The second crab was in the side yard, turning to the sound of their attempted escape. Without hesitation, it darted with pincers open.

Val ducked back inside.

"Into the basement!"

"The basement?!" Alan said. "We'll be trapped down there!"

The sight of the two claws piercing the backdoor swiftly ended that debate. Behind them, the other crab had squeezed in through the front entrance and was now heading toward the kitchen.

Reality sunk in. They had no choice except to make a last stand at the basement.

"The basement will do." Alan was the first into the hallway. Taylor and Val were right behind him, the latter knocking the kitchen table into the crab's path. It tore at the inedible piece of furniture as though it were a mortal enemy. Val followed Taylor into the stairway and slammed the door shut behind him.

Another reality sank in: that door would not hold.

He had to think fast. Bullets obviously didn't work against those things. Outrunning them was unlikely to work. Barricading the door would only delay the inevitable for a few minutes at most. No way would they be able to drive it away physically, which left only chemical alternatives.

The pointed legs tore up the tile as the crab entered the hall.

Val went with the only option he could think of. He ran down the steps to the laundry machine. He reached into the cabinet and grabbed a jug of bleach, then raced back up the steps.

"What are you doing?!" Taylor shouted.

Val ignored her and reached the top step, unscrewing the cap. He swallowed, told himself how stupid he was for attempting this, then opened the door.

The crab was right there, its claws primed and ready to snatch him up.

A white liquid splashed its face. Its arms coiled back, the claws attempting to brush the unfamiliar substance from its eyes and mouth. White bubbles foamed over its mandibles.

It backed away from the door, giving Val space to step into the hall and splash it again.

By then, the second one had made its way into the kitchen.

Val splashed the nearest crab a second time, driving it back further. The plan was effective. Unfortunately, his ammo was already low. The jug was half-full to start with, and now there was only a little bit left.

With the second crab advancing, he went with the only plan he could think of. He dumped most of the remaining bleach near the doorway, forming a chemical barrier. Next, he threw the jug at the second crab, which reacted violently when its contents splashed its right eye.

Val ducked back inside and shut the door. He slowly backed down the stairs, listening to the ruckus outside. The crabs approached, then paused.

Several tense moments followed.

Alright, come on. If you guys are gonna come after us, just get it over with!

They clicked their mandibles and scraped the wet floor with their claws. Slowly, they began backing away into the kitchen.

The calm was replaced by chaos. Plywood and marble was bashed as the crabs began ransacking the kitchen. They ripped the door off the refrigerator and spilled its contents onto the floor. A second phase of relative calmness followed, during which Val realized they were probably scavenging off the lunchmeat. That assumption was backed up with the sound of the pantry being raided. Cans of chili and green beans exploded, cereal spilled, and pasta jars shattered.

Val moved to the bottom of the steps, then took a seat on the sofa.

"Now I'm *really* overdue for a grocery trip."

CHAPTER 19

"Come on, dispatch. Anybody? Hello?!"

Val sat on the sofa, his head in his hand. He wasn't sure which was more aggravating: the pounding in his head or Alan Goldstein's nonstop attempts to get a call out. It seemed the guy could not get over the fact that his phone and radio were drenched in the lake. That was the price for not having a case, something Val was tempted to say. He held back. Now wasn't the time. After all, it wasn't every day you nearly get killed by giant radioactive crabs. Also, they had just lost a fellow officer. While Val didn't have the greatest opinion of Alan—he was a bully and a prick—this wasn't something he felt the guy deserved.

"Alan, give it up already," Taylor said. She was knelt by a space heater, which finally managed to dry her uniform after two hours. She stood up, her clothes feeling much lighter than before.

She turned to Val. "My mind's been so busy, I just realized I didn't thank you for letting us in."

He smirked then waved his hand dismissively. "No need to thank me for that. What was I gonna do? Leave you to get killed by those things?"

"No, but you probably postponed it," Alan said. He was by the stairs listening to the movement above. The crabs had finished ransacking the place. So far, they had not made an effort to approach the basement door. Either they were deterred by the bleach, or they had just forgotten about the fresh meat below.

They weren't making nearly as much noise as before. Once in a while, they would hear one moving across the kitchen or living room. One of them had toppled the loveseat earlier, possibly believing it to be edible.

One thing was certain: they were still in the house.

"Any chance someone will come looking for you?" Val asked.

"Maybe, but they won't know where to look," Taylor said. "We came by boat. Stopped by after we saw the wrecks in your driveway. They came out of the water and pulled us down."

"The boat might still be visible in the daylight," Alan said. "But in the dead of night? No way they'll see it. Assuming anyone even comes looking. They probably still think we're at the creek."

"They came in through the creek?" Val asked. Taylor nodded. "So they are from Lake Alocasia?!" "You figured it out too?"

"I had time on my hands," Val said. "After what happened with Robin, I was researching freshwater crabs, then learned that they had infiltrated that lake. Add the nuclear waste, and I did the math."

"The only math I'm interested in is how fast can we get the hell out of here," Alan said.

"You saw how fast they are," Val said. "You wanna try outrunning them? You won't get far."

"Oh, so staying down here is your plan? Is that what you were doing before?"

"More or less," Val said. "I had a rough night myself, hence the truck in my driveway." He noticed Taylor looking at him inquisitively. "Robin's psycho ex-boyfriend. You met him at the Bowen property. Somehow he tracked me down, and… well…" He mimicked a few haymakers, then pointed to the sound of crab feet moving above them.

Alan sat on the bottom step, completely focused on listening for the crustaceans. The sound of movement came to a stop. Silence took over.

"I don't think they're in the kitchen," he said.

"Doesn't mean they've left the house," Val said.

"We're gonna have to do something," Alan said. "It won't be long before they break down that door."

"Where would we go?" Taylor asked. "We don't have a vehicle."

Val thought for a moment. "My neighbor's house. He's out of town at the moment. He left me his house key because I was doing some electrical work around his property."

"Okay, sounds good," Alan said, guardedly. "But what's to keep these bastards from following us in? Does he have a car or something over there?"

"No, but he does have a landline. We can call someone."

"Great!" Alan stood up. "Then what are we waiting for? We can make it."

"Wait." Val stepped after him. "Stop freaking out, dude. You go up there, you'll get crabbed before you're out of the hall."

"Listen!" Alan pointed up and waited. They stood still for over a minute. There was not a single sound coming from above. "I think they've gone."

"We don't know that."

"I'm not staying down here forever," Alan said. "You guys wanna stay, that's fine. Me, I'm gone." He planted his foot on the top step and began his ascent.

"Wait!" Val grabbed him by the shoulder and pulled him back. Alan turned and pushed him away. Val approached a second time. "You open that door, and they're still out there, then we're all dead."

Alan started backing up the steps. "Stay back, man."

Val did not abide. He came at him again, grabbing him by the collar with both hands.

"You're not going out there."

Alan replied with a headbutt. For what felt like the millionth time, Val took a blow to the noggin. The throbbing pain briefly amplified tenfold, causing his grip to loosen. Alan shoved him backwards once more, then placed his hand on his sidearm.

Backing up the steps, he looked to Taylor. "You coming?"

She hurried to Val's side, checking his head. She looked at Alan with disgust. He was a flawed man for sure, but she never knew him to be this cavalier.

"Don't go, Alan. You'll get yourself killed."

Alan shrugged. "Have it your way."

He went up the steps, not looking back as he opened the door. The door swung inward, unveiling the crab waiting on the other side.

Alan froze, caught in complete surprise at the big disc-shape with spider-like legs coiled on each side.

Impelled by his presence, it stood up, matching his height.

He turned to run, falling forward as it seized his ankle. His jaw came down on one of the steps, uprooting one of his crowns. Spitting blood, he tried crawling away.

Right away, it started pulling him up the stairs.

"Help me! Help me!"

Val and Taylor raced up the steps and grabbed his outstretched hands. The crab halted, surprised to see the competition for its meal. Its claw remained latched on Alan's leg, its other closing over his shin.

Alan reared his head back, his teeth clenched and eyes wide.

"It's breaking my leg! It's breaking my leg—AHHH!"

The breaking of bone was loud and gut-wrenching.

Taylor drew her pistol and blasted at the crab. It flinched, still maintaining its grasp. She tried to go for the eyes, but missed the small, wavering targets.

Their ears now ringing, they resorted to outmuscling the crab.

It let go with one claw and lashed out, grabbing Alan by his buttocks. He shrieked as the bony appendage tore into the soft flesh.

"AH! AH! AH!"

Alan used his free arm to unholster his sidearm and point it at the crab.

His first shot struck the edge of its head, exploding into shards, one of which flew back right into Val's left shoulder. Sudden pain severed his grip on Alan's wrist, dooming the officer to be pulled through the doorway and out of sight. Alan screamed and babbled, shooting his gun until it ran empty.

"Get off! Get—AH! AH! AH! WAHHHH—ehhhhh!"

Val stepped into the hallway just in time to see Alan get flayed open. He was still reaching for Val's hand, even as his intestines were getting pulled from his abdomen.

The second crab emerged from the living room area and joined the meal. It went for Alan's broken leg, easily separating it from the knee.

Taylor stepped out, then dry-heaved when seeing her partner disemboweled. She was quickly pushed back through the door by Val.

"Can't help him. Hurry. Go!"

He shut the door behind them and followed Taylor down the stairs. For the next few seconds, they were forced to listen to Alan's gargled screams. After a few seconds, he went silent, and all they could hear was the sound of tearing and slurping.

Taylor sank onto the sofa.

"You alright?" Val said.

She shook her head. After wiping a tear from her eye, she looked to the doorway.

"He wasn't completely wrong. It's just a matter of time before they get in here."

Val nodded.

Taylor examined her magazine. Only six rounds remained. It may as well have been zero, since nine-millimeters were absolutely useless against the crabs.

She holstered the weapon, then took a deep breath to calm herself.

There was a crackling sound from bones breaking, then suddenly, another gargled scream.

"Eh…eh… EHHH!"

Taylor tucked her head down and pressed her hands over her ears. Alan wasn't dead yet.

"He—eelppp—BLECH!"

There was an intense sound of fluid hitting the kitchen floor. It didn't take much imagination to know he was vomiting blood.

Taylor passed out against the arm of the sofa.

Val checked to make sure she didn't hit her head, then laid her flat on the furniture.

After a few minutes, the gargling came to a definitive stop.

Val began to pace around the basement. A certain fact now occupied his mind.

Once those crabs were done feeding, they would certainly come for them.

CHAPTER 20

Today was the big day.

Normally, Arthur Bowen would spend his mornings sipping coffee on the front porch while keeping up with the news. That was how he would prefer to spend this Saturday morning, but instead, he was trying to fit into his old tux.

Leslie's desire for an early morning wedding was something he would never understand. Nine o'clock was coming fast. The groom, Dale Woods, was already dressed up and wandering around the yard. The lawn had been freshly mowed and smelled of cut grass. It was also a mistake, as the clippings mixed with the morning dew. Everyone who walked on the lawn now had grass clinging to their shoes.

Hopefully by nine, most of it would have evaporated, but during the prep, everyone was shaking their feet trying to get the stuff off. Arthur made a decision to wear his boots in the meantime, even though he remained on the porch.

He could hear Leslie upstairs, whining to one of her bridesmaids.

Probably about her dress.

Wanda stepped out. Arthur did a double take, surprised at the amount of cleavage her dress showed off.

"Well, hot damn, honey!"

Wanda smiled. "You like it, huh?"

"Trying to win the groom over or something?"

Her smile disappeared. "And here I was thinking you were being charming. How foolish of me."

"Well, it's just that…" Arthur decided to keep his opinion to himself. Unfortunately for him, that decision came a few seconds too late.

"'It's just that' what, exactly?" she said.

"Nothing." He pretended to watch the DJs set up their stuff. "Don't know why they're in such a hurry. The actual party doesn't start until one."

"Don't change the subject," Wanda said. "What were you about to say?"

Arthur looked at his coffee, which no longer looked appealing. He turned around and marched inside. Wanda followed him into the kitchen, where he began preparing a mimosa.

"I was gonna say you look gorgeous," he said.

"Right. That's why you cut yourself off," she said.

The lawyer in Arthur screamed. How could he make such a dumb argument? Like a rookie, he dug a trap for himself.

"Will you just let it go? You look great. Just take the compliment and shut up." He walked past her with his drink and leaned on the patio fence to watch the setup. His first sip turned into a guzzle as Wanda followed him out.

"Just say it!"

Arthur swallowed, then gave her a glare. He eyed the cleavage, then shrugged. "Alright. Fine. You're… a little long in the tooth for that kind of outfit."

The glass was slapped out of his hand.

"I don't know why I married an asshole like you!"

"I know why." Arthur took his wallet out of his pocket, then stuffed it back in. "Also why you *stayed* married to me. Or rather, the prenup is why."

This time, she smacked him across the face. The action attracted the attention of most of the wedding party and staff.

Wanda marched into the house, slamming the door behind her.

The DJ quickly stepped forward. "Is everything okay, Mr. Bowen?"

Quarter Horse. Even after spending several days with this moron, Arthur still didn't know why he went with that name. On the other hand, perhaps he didn't want to know. It didn't matter. Arthur had already come up with his own explanation: *Because he's a moron.*

He pointed at his glass. "It will be once I have a refill." He looked at his watch. "Be even better in twenty-four hours. Then I'll finally have all this crap out of my yard."

"Don't worry, sir," Quarter Horse said. "We'll make sure there's no mess after the party."

Arthur snorted, then nodded at the cords, folding chairs, and flowers. Already, a few people had dropped trash all over the place. Several people were bitching to each other about the grass clippings on their shoes and ankles. The pastor was running late, as were some of the guests.

He shut his eyes and reminded himself that there was still an hour to go.

It's not like it's the end of the world.

"HEY! IT'S TOO TIGHT!" Leslie yelled from upstairs.

"I'm sorry, I'm sorry," her bridesmaid said.

His meditative effort came to a crashing end. Arthur stepped onto the lawn and picked up his glass.

"I know how I'm spending the next morning."

"Don't worry, sir. I doubt it'll get too bad," Quarter Horse said.

"Not off to a good start," Arthur said.

"Aw, come on." The DJ laughed. "How bad can it get?"

Arthur ignored him and returned inside for his refill. As soon as he was through the door, he was met with another glare from his wife.

That is the question, isn't it? How bad can this morning really get?

CHAPTER 21

"Shh, shh, relax. Take it slow."

Val put a hand on Taylor's shoulder as she stirred. She looked around, initially appearing confused, then quickly looking disappointed. For a moment, she thought that the last eight hours had been a dream.

"How long was I out?"

"For quite a while," Val said. "It's morning now."

Taylor looked up the stairway. The door was still intact, but she could hear motion in the kitchen and hallway.

"What have they been doing?"

"They fed on Alan for an hour after you passed out," Val said. "Then they settled down. I hate to phrase it this way, but I think they took a nap."

"Shouldn't they return to the water?" she said.

"I've read some crabs can survive out of water for a couple of days," Val said. "To be honest, I think they don't want to abandon their next meal... *Us.*"

Taylor already felt she might pass out again.

"Sorry," Val said.

"No, it's alright." She sat up and regained control of herself. Again, there was more movement upstairs.

A scrape against the door made her jump from the sofa.

"The hell? Did they wait for me to wake up to decide to break in and kill us?"

"That adds up," Val muttered.

In his mind, it did. Those damn things take their sweet time killing their prey, devouring them slowly with no mind to the pain of their victims. From what he understood through documentaries and articles, most species killed their prey before eating it. Usually, if something was eaten alive, it was either swallowed whole, or the predator was unable to kill it before feeding. That was often the case with lions. Primarily, they killed their prey first. However, if something was too big, a young elephant perhaps, they sometimes could not bite the jugular. Even crocodiles and sharks tended to kill their prey relatively quick, depending on the situation. Hyenas often ate their victims alive, but that was usually due to fierce competition in the pack. Komodo dragons were probably the most vicious predators he had read about. They wore their prey down with a venomous bite, then often beat them into the ground before consuming.

Their ferocity paled to that of the crabs. They severed limbs and removed innards, all while their victim suffered. Though Val did not suspect the crabs to be intelligent, he did find it peculiar how violent their mutation had made them. Even carnivorous crabs of normal size were scavengers above all else. Not these big ones. They seemed to enjoy juicy flesh above all else.

A harder impact shook the door. The next hit splintered the center.

Val and Taylor stood in the middle of the basement. There was nowhere to run to, nowhere to hide. The intruder proceeded to smash the door like a slasher villain, even peeking through the breach with its black eye.

Taylor raised a middle finger to it.

The crab watched for a moment, then struck again. An eighteen-inch slab of wood broke free and skipped down the steps.

"I think you pissed it off," Val said.

"How are we gonna get out of here?" Taylor said. "I'm open to suggestions."

"I'm thinking."

"Think fast." Taylor looked at the cabinet above the washer and dryer. "I don't suppose you have any more bleach."

"No, just—" A realization came to mind. He dashed for the washer unit and dug through the cabinets above it. After brushing aside a few items, he located a green box with an illustration of a blue cannister and black bugs.

"Bug bomb?" Taylor said.

"They don't like chemicals. If you have any better ideas…"

A fourth hit broke the top half of the door off.

Taylor snatched the box from his hand and opened it. There were three cannisters inside. The instructions were simple: break the seal and press all the way down on the valve.

They ran up the stairs, stopping just out of reach of the pincers. Holding his foggers like hand grenades, Val pressed down on the valve. The cannisters hissed as they released their contents.

Val tossed them through the gap in the door, then hugged the wall as Taylor tossed hers.

The crab withdrew its pincer, then snapped at the weird substance billowing around it. After a few moments, it backed away, right into its brethren. The two crabs began snapping their claws at each other, neither one able to penetrate the other's shell.

A grey cloud quickly filled the hallway and kitchen. The crabs ceased their quarrel, then snapped at the air again. Their motions became increasingly frantic as the poison embodied them. The fog stung their eyes and dried their mouths.

Their need to feed was replaced by a need to return to the lake.

Val and Taylor waited downstairs, listening to the crabs retreat into the living room. There was a brief pause in their escape, caused by an intense ruckus. Val couldn't help but smirk. The crabs were fighting again, likely because they tried to exit the door at the same time.

His smile vanished after he saw the cloud rolling down the steps.

"Oh shit."

Taylor covered her mouth. "Should we wait, or…"

"Nope. This is our chance."

"What the hell are we waiting for then?"

Taylor was the first up the steps. Val was right on her heels, holding his breath as they arrived in the hall.

They made their way through the blinding cloud, stumbling over the ruins of the ransacked kitchen.

Taylor winced, feeling the wet sensation of Alan's blood under her heel. She ignored it and pressed on. They escaped through the widened back doorway, taking a much welcomed deep breath of fresh air.

"This way," Val said, pointing north.

They ran across the driveway toward a small section of woods that separated Val's house from his neighbor's. As they went, they looked to the lake, just in time to see the two crabs enter the water—and for the third to make eye contact with them.

Water dripped from its shell as it stepped ashore, the crab having spent the morning hours in the shallows.

"Go!" Val shouted.

They penetrated the group of trees, hopping over roots and branches as they made their way to the other side. They arrived on Charles Netty's property, glancing back at the sound of devastation behind them.

Like an eight-legged bulldozer, the crab railroaded any obstacle in its path. Branches were splintered, bushes were flattened, and any critters in the vicinity retreated with angst.

Val and Taylor raced across the yard. Already, fatigue was working against them. It had been a long night, and Val was still aching from the heavy beating by William Cook's posse.

The crab emerged from the trees, its speed immediately doubling out in the open.

Val fumbled with his keys, searching for the one Charles had given him.

"Crap! Crap! Crap!"

Taylor pressed her back to the front door, aiming her Glock at the oncoming crab. "Anytime now, Val!"

"I'm trying!"

"You have enough keys?!"

"Sorry for not anticipating a killer crab invasion when I started my business!"

The crab was a dozen feet away.

Taylor groaned through her teeth, doing everything she could to keep her wits intact. She steadied her hands as best she could, then squeezed the trigger.

Splat!

The crab came to a sudden halt, dripping black goo from its exploded eyeball. Half-blind and caught off guard, the crab spun in a circle, slashing its claws wildly.

Taylor gasped, amazed at herself for pulling off the shot.

"Over here!" Val said.

He led her to the shed in the backyard. The door was secured by a padlock. Val yanked on it futilely for a moment before looking to the deputy.

"Mind shooting that off?"

Taylor didn't bother asking him what the plan was. A single shot took the padlock right off. She was glad she didn't waste time asking questions, for the answer became obvious when the doors swung open. On the left side was a gas-powered lawnmower and a four-gallon gas can.

Val grabbed the can and unscrewed the top. As he dumped the contents into a bucket, he gave a glance to the crab. Its moment of panic had ceased, though it was still a bit confused. It went for the door where its prey had been standing, finding nothing there. It turned toward the sound of movement, locating them with its good eye.

With all four gallons in the bucket, Val grabbed a box of long-reach matches from a shelf.

"Val, don't! You'll get too close!" Taylor said.

Val shoved the matches into her hand. "Light the whole box." Without waiting to make sure she understood, he lifted the gasoline bucket and went on a collision course with the crab.

Seeing its prey nearly within reach, it opened its pincers, eager to satisfy its unrelenting hunger.

Instead of meat, it tasted chemicals and petroleum. Its exploded eye stung intensely, causing the crab's senses to go haywire.

Val splashed the rest of the gasoline onto the crustacean, thoroughly smothering it. He dropped the empty bucket and darted out of the way.

"Taylor, *now!*"

She lit one of the matches, then stuck the head into the top of the box, lighting all of the other matchheads. Now, she held a blazing torch in her hand.

The crab ceased its flailing, its emotionless eye fixed on her.

"Sorry. I'm all out of butter."

She threw the torch, igniting the crab on impact. Burning mandibles and limbs flailed wildly. The crab teetered on its back legs, claws lashing at the air. It spun in circles, unsure of what to do. Its remaining eye blistered, then exploded. Its internal temperature spiked to five-hundred degrees. The moisture inside its shell evaporated into gas, which desperately searched for a place to escape. That place was the chitin in its joints. Little ruptures burst like party balloons, spewing boiling fluid.

The crab darted several feet into the yard, trailing smoke. Like a tiny meteor, it dripped smoldering fluid and waste, which scorched the grass below.

Finally, it slowed to a stop, then slumped on its face. Its legs twitched, then stiffened.

Taylor and Val leaned against each other and took in a deep breath. The crab was dead.

They spent the next minute watching it burn. It was simultaneously a sight of horror and awe. The flames were starting to die down, leaving behind a charred shell with shriveled insides.

Slowly, but truly, the adrenaline rush began to subside.

Val dug his keys out of his pocket, then smirked. "Here it is." He isolated the correct key and held it up. Taylor chuckled, then walked beside him to the door.

A blast of air conditioning hit them as they stepped inside. The living room was basic, with a three-cushion couch near the front window, and a recliner chair opposite it. Farther back was the kitchen.

Immediately, they went for the sink and filled two glasses with water. Never before had well water tasted so good.

The landline was on the wall near the dining room table. Taylor, now adequately rehydrated, began dialing the station.

"Hi, this is Deputy Taylor Davies. I'm calling from the property of Charles Netty. I need units here right away."

As Taylor informed her department, Val helped himself to the fridge. With the tension alleviated for the moment, his appetite had somewhat returned. He rolled up some lunchmeat and cheese, then stuffed it in his mouth. It was all he needed for right now. On the bottom shelf were a few water bottles. He tossed one to Taylor, then took another to the living room, where he collapsed on the sofa.

He leaned against the soft pillow, and shut his eyes. Relief and angst acted as two opposing forces in a battle for his sensibilities. On the one hand, he could not stop thinking of Robin. Her horrible death was still front and center in his memory, as was the guilt he felt.

In contrast, knowing he had killed one of the crabs partially alleviated that guilt. It was only one crab out of at least three, and he couldn't be sure if it was the one that killed Robin. At the very least, its death meant less people would suffer.

Then there were the other two. The last he saw, they had retreated to the lake. Val wondered if they took in enough of the poison to die. Then again, they would have had to breath it in. He had heard that some crabs had duel respiration, allowing them to breath on land and in water. Maybe the other two were suffering at the bottom of the lake. Maybe he had killed all of them.

The distant sound of fluttering wings broke his train of thought.

Val opened his eyes and saw a family of geese taking flight, dripping water onto the lawn. The water where they floated started to swirl.

Oh, no. Please, God. Not again...

The two crabs emerged from the shallows. Uprooted weeds covered their bodies, giving them a swampy, ghoulish appearance. Side-by-side, they raced up the shore...

...Directly at the house.

Val was on his feet. "Taylor!"

"...Yeah, that's the correct address... hang on..." She looked at him. "What?... OH SHIT!!!" A lakeview window near the dining room table provided the answer to her question.

Rehydrated and rejuvenated, the crabs marched to the house, likely drawn by the smoke.

Val slammed the door shut. It was an action done purely out of instinct. He remembered how useless doors were when the claws punched through. A few hits reduced the door to a pile of splinters.

Too wide for the doorway, one of the crabs began ripping at the frames. Meanwhile, the second one went around to the front of the house, where it spotted its meals through the window.

SMASH!

Glass shrapnel rained onto the living room carpet, making way for the big crustacean.

Val and Taylor backed into the kitchen.

The crab followed, its legs tearing up the carpet and kitchen tile. Huge black claws remained tucked by the carapace, like the arms of a praying mantis. A slimy string of saliva dripped from the mouthparts, like drool from a starving canine eyeing a helpless critter.

Behind it, more wood and drywall was flung into the living room as the other crab continued to hack away. Being single-minded in its attempt to breach, it took no notice of the large window its counterpart entered through.

Taylor and Val stepped around the kitchen island, then followed a hall to the backdoor.

The crab arrived at the island, and with a single motion, uprooted it with its claws and tossed it aside.

Taylor extended her pistol in hopes of hitting it in the eye. All four rounds missed their mark, instead fracturing against its rigid shell. Taylor looked at the locked slide on her pistol. She had no ammo. Worse, she had no ideas on how to escape. Perhaps her fellow police officers would arrive in time.

More than ever, Taylor understood the value of a fast response time.

"Out this way," Val said. "There's a back door."

They went through the hall and out the door. It was a sliding glass door, more than wide enough for their pursuer to burst through—which it did.

Glass exploded onto the lawn. The beast scurried outside, a mere six feet behind its intended victims.

"Good GOD!" Taylor shouted. In sheer desperation, she chucked her empty firearm. The beast took no notice of the weapon bouncing over its shell as it continued its pursuit.

The chase continued around the back of the house toward the driveway. At this point, all they knew to do was run away. Fatigue proved that was a faulty plan that would only lead to death. Both of them were gasping for breath, while the crabs showed no signs of slowing down. Simple-minded creatures, completely void of emotion, they were not worn down by a night of stress and anxiety. Their only discomfort was the pain of hunger.

As they entered the driveway, Taylor stumbled, her foot having caught on the trench Val had dug. He turned and caught her, preventing a fall.

Val looked to the cables he had laid out, then at the juncture he had recently attached them to.

An idea came to mind.

"Look out!" Taylor shouted, pushing him away. They went in opposite directions, briefly confusing the crab. It turned one way, then the other, unsure of which direction it wanted to go.

Taking advantage of its hesitation, Val doubled back to the shed. Like a crazy looter, he began digging through all of Charles's tools.

Taylor stopped in the side yard, watching him disappear inside.

"What are you doing?" She immediately regretted shouting. Not only did she gain the attention of her pursuer, but the second crab as well. It had finally widened the front doorway, only to find its target out in the open.

They came at her from different directions. Taylor stepped back, breathing shakily. Sweat dripped from her face, her police gear never feeling heavier.

At this moment, it felt like the end had come. She had come so close, only to be slaughtered now.

Her sense of defeat subsided when Val reappeared. In his hand was a can of what appeared to be a spray. He ran as close as he could, stopping in the driveway. He brought his arm back like an MLB pitcher, then tossed it to her.

Taylor had to step forward to grab it, putting her dangerously close to the crabs. She immediately backpedaled, narrowly avoiding one of the snapping claws. The crab tried again and again. *SNAP! SNAP! SNAP!* Each attempt was inches from reach.

She gave the can a quick glance. Wasp Aerosol Sprayer. She shook the can and blasted its contents. The stinging chemicals stopped the crabs in their tracks. Just as they did in the bug bomb cloud, they began snapping wildly, their senses haywire.

The one on her left, blinded by the sand-colored liquid, stumbled into its companion.

For the second time, the misunderstanding sparked a brawl. The crab turned and grabbed the other by the leg. Edged pincers sliced the chitin tissue in the joints, sparking pain.

The two bodies became a writhing blur of pincers and legs. Creatures of equal strength and resolve, they struggled to outmatch each other. Only one had the advantage.

The crab with the injured leg struggled to maintain its footing. Its brethren—now its mortal enemy—pressed its attack, violently snapping at its face. After numerous lunges, it managed to seize a mandible. A relatively thin appendage, it easily snapped off under the might of the large pincer.

Before it could register the pain of its missing mouth part, the crab suffered the anguish of one its eyes being snapped off. Half-blind, the injured crab attempted to back away, dripping blood from its mouth and eye.

Its opponent was not finished. It charged, its lashing claws easily getting past the defenses. With a snap of the white pincers, the other eye was gone.

Now completely blind, the crab was in a frenzy. It snapped its claws recklessly, hoping to fend off its foe.

The next attack came from the side. Seized by its rear left legs, the injured crab was flipped on its back. It flailed like a bug seized in a spider's web, kicking and squirming. Those eight legs went from squirming to tensing as the pincers penetrated the softer underbelly shell.

Water and bodily fluids bubbled as shell fragments were torn away, revealing the juicy flesh underneath. The tension increased as the pincers ripped into the meat. Stomach, intestines, gills, heart—all of it was ripe for the taking.

With long, raking motions, the attacker turned its enemies insides into minced meat.

From where Val stood, the crabs looked like a pair of humongous ants fighting in a colonial war. The loser stiffened, twitching slightly as the winner fed on its entrails. While the crabs did not go out of their way to be cannibalistic, they had no qualms about feeding on their dead members.

Not that Val was complaining. The wasp spray had worked better than he anticipated. He hoped for Taylor to stall the creatures. Instead, she ignited a fight to the death.

Two down, one to go.

Sprinting as fast as she could, she joined him by the shed.

"You alright?" he asked.

"Better than that sucker," she said, tilting her head at the dead crab. The victor backed away from its meal and turned in their direction. Taylor groaned, thinking it would be distracted enough for them to get away. Perhaps human meat tasted better than crab meat. Whatever the reason was, it was advancing on them with intent to kill.

Val held up a folding chair taken from the shed. "Pray this works?"

"What? You gonna go all WrestleMania on it?" she said.

"No. Just set it up for a little shock."

With that said, he ran to the driveway and set the chair up near the trench. Using both hands, he raised the piece of pipe which contained the cable. It was heavy, but adrenaline gave him the extra strength he needed. He centered it on the folding chair, then crouched behind it.

"Come on, you big clam! Open those claws wide! Come on!" He slapped the pipe, egging the crab further.

It doubled its speed and raised its claws.

Val tensed, waiting until the last possible moment to jump away. He would need precise timing with no margin for error.

Oh God, this is stupid...

The crab closed the distance and lunged at him with its claws.

At that moment, Val dove to the ground and covered his head.

Snap!

The crab never knew what it had grabbed. Snapping with incredible force, the claws easily sliced through the piping, into the live cables. An electrical surge shook its body relentlessly. Sparks flew and smoke billowed into long grey towers.

Slowly, Val crawled away, not daring to look back. Taylor rushed to his side and helped him to his feet. Only when he was at the shed did he finally look at the shuddering crustacean.

It convulsed for nearly two minutes, its legs and arms moving in slow, tense motions the entire time. The fur on its claws ignited into flame. Finally, the electrical surge contracted its muscles enough for the pincers to squeeze harder. The cable snapped completely, the two halves falling to the ground.

The crab stood like a black statue, its mitten claws now black and rigid as the rest of its body. It remained as still as a

Greek statue, its eyes fixed on the two humans standing before it.

Its legs buckled under its own weight. The crab collapsed, its life having reached its shocking conclusion.

Val and Taylor were the next to collapse. In their case, it was from pure exhaustion. Taylor leaned her head on his shoulder. There was never any understanding of affection between the two of them. But after a night of unrelenting horror and bloodshed, she needed to feel close to someone. She was pleased that Val did not stop her.

Blaring sirens echoed from the long driveway, growing steadily louder until three police SUVs arrived in the driveway.

The sheriff was the first to step out, subsequently making him the first to freeze at the alarming sight of giant crabs on the property. The other deputies joined him, each mumbling the same phrase.

"What the fuck?"

Val leaned his head against Taylor's. Something about it felt right in this moment.

"Well, at least help finally arrived."

Despite the loss of friends and the unfathomable terror they endured, they both managed to chuckle at his joke. It was another thing that felt right in this moment.

CHAPTER 22

Seated in lawn chairs taken from Charles Netty's shed, Val and Taylor finished giving their debriefing. The presence of these large crustaceans gave the Sheriff a whole new understanding of what happened with Robin Berry. All doubts were eliminated. It was evident he was telling the truth.

The energy on this 'crime scene' was low and somber. Word had spread through the department that Deputies Alan Goldstein and Simon Heather were dead.

Val did not envy the Sheriff his duty of informing the family members, especially the parents. How could one explain that a loved one was devoured by giant crabs? Even worse, there were hardly any remains to be put to rest. There would be no coffin, not even a cremation. Just a headstone looking over some grass.

HAZMAT crews were on the scene, erecting barriers around each crab corpse. Geiger counters were employed to get readings on the creatures. The results were overwhelming.

"Yeah, Sheriff, we've got a positive reading," one of the crewmembers said. "Frankly, I'm surprised these bastards aren't glowing."

"No. Just really big," the Sheriff said.

Val watched as a patrol boat cruised near the east shoreline. Another boat was checking a lakefront property across the lake further to the north. From the look of it, the police were discovering evidence of more victims by the hour. He could hear through the police radios that other officers were searching by the neck of the lake. With all those coves, there were numerous places for other crabs to hide.

"Sheriff, the end of this dock over here is FUBAR. Looks like the crabs paid the homeowner a visit at one point."

"Copy that."

"My God," Taylor said. "We're gonna need to close this lake. We can't let anyone swim here."

"I know, I know. But it might be over," the Sheriff said. "Thanks to you two."

"But if there's more…"

"We're figuring that out right now," the Sheriff said. "I've called the council-manager. We're gonna get a statement out to the public. Remember, Lake Lucas is big. It's hard to get word to all the fishermen and campers, especially with all the dead zones around here." He tapped their shoulders reassuringly. "Sorry for all you guys went through. Just try and relax, alright?"

"Don't have to tell me twice," Val said.

A few moments of peace and quiet passed, during which the two survivors sipped on bottled water. The other deputies offered coffee, but the last thing either of them wanted right now was a caffeine rush.

"What's gonna happen with you?" Taylor said.

"Hmm?"

"Your business. Your career. You planning on staying?"

Val watched the lake for a moment before answering.

"I don't know. Considering everything that happened here, I suspect business will slow down for the next few years. I might have to consider relocating. On the other hand, I've grown to love this place."

"Maybe there's a middle ground," Taylor said. "Keep this place, while conducting business elsewhere."

"That's a thought." Val rested his chin on his palm. "That said, it'll be hard to start somewhere new. It seems wherever I go, my reputation follows me. No matter how hard I try, my past always seems to track me down."

Taylor put a hand on his shoulder. "Then you carve out a new future."

Val looked over at her. Her gentle gaze was soothing to the soul. He remembered when he first came to this town. Everyone kept a distance. Many refused to even make eye contact. Even clerks at grocery and hardware stores seemed reluctant to engage with him.

Taylor was one of the few who didn't look at him with suspicion. At first, he thought she was simply oblivious to his background. However, even when it became clear she knew of his crimes, she treated him like a human being.

Perhaps it was the dopamine they felt from narrowly surviving the crab encounter. Perhaps it was their exhausted minds looking for some kind of comfort. Or, maybe it was something real.

Regardless, they were enjoying this moment of silent affection.

An alarmed voice coming through the police radio brought that moment to an end.

"Sheriff! This is Unit Four."

"I'm here," the Sheriff replied.

"Sir, we just found a boat in the neck of the lake. Specifically, one of the coves. There's a bunch of gear inside, but nobody on it."

"Did anyone see it on the way up here?"

"It was wedged under some thick canopy. Easy to miss if you weren't specifically looking for it. And sir, there's dried up bait, warm beer, and food items in here. I think it has been here for a couple days at least."

"Oh, Jesus," the Sheriff muttered.

"Thank God they're dead," one of the other deputies said.

Val's throat tightened. "That's further north."

"Yeah," the Sheriff said. "They must've trekked up there, then came back."

"But…" he looked to Taylor. "Didn't you find evidence that they entered through Lake Alocasia?" She nodded. "They were migrating north. Why would they go through the neck of the lake, into busier territory, only to double-back?"

The answer was obvious.

Taylor stood up. "There's more of them."

The Sheriff put his hands up. "Okay, let's not panic. Most of that area is fairly deep. There's no coves, and there's a plain line of sight. Unless there's some large gathering, I don't think we have to… worry…" Hearing himself speak, he remembered a particular gathering that was taking place. "Aw, shit."

"The Bowen wedding," Val said. "We gotta go!"

"This way." Taylor ran to the nearest deputy. "Hey, you planning to stay and monitor this area?"

"Yeah…"

"Good! I need your keys."

She snatched the key from his hand and ran to the SUV. As she started the engine, she heard the passenger door open. Val climbed into the passenger seat and slammed the door shut.

"Need me to ride in the back?"

"You don't have to come at all."

"No, I need to see this through," he said.

Rather than waste time arguing, Taylor did a U-turn and raced out of the driveway. As they arrived at the road, the Sheriff's voice began blasting through the radio.

"I need units assembled on the north end of Lake Lucas. Dispatch, alert the SWAT team and the State Police. Get a call to Arthur Bowen's phone immediately and warn him to cancel his event."

Val couldn't help but scoff. "Yeah, I'm sure that'll go over well."

CHAPTER 23

"Thank you for being here with us today as we witness the lifelong union of Leslie Bowen and Dale Woods. Today, we celebrate the separate journeys that brought them together, and we usher them toward the new journey they will embark upon together."

Arthur Bowen sat in the front row alongside his wife. He groaned audibly, feeling his phone buzzing against his hip for the third time. He had no idea who was trying to call him, nor did he care.

As the officiant began the service, Arthur tried to focus on his daughter's happiness. Despite his griping leading up to today, there was no denying he felt a touch of emotion when walking her down the makeshift aisle. Leslie maintained a wide smile, even when smelling a touch of bourbon on his breath. Her concerns were alleviated when he completed the walk without embarrassing himself.

The bourbon was necessary. After all, nothing else would dull the pain of sitting next to the monster that married his wallet. Sure, Wanda took his name and bore his child. It was the price she was willing to pay… for a while.

Her smile was somewhere between genuine and forced. Whenever she focused on the ceremony, it leaned toward genuine. It became more strained the longer Arthur sat next to her. She could smell the bourbon and cigar tobacco in his breath and on his suit. Arthur knew there would be words later, but he didn't care. Part of him was tempted to sever ties with the wench. She barely put out nowadays, and frankly, he wasn't sure if he wanted her to..

She's quite the far cry from the dame I married.

The fact that he was willing to acknowledge it was telling in itself. As he had previously reminded Wanda, he had the prenuptial agreement. He would have no problem scoring a younger, more obedient partner. On plenty of occasions, he had been asked by blondes as young as nineteen "how's your wife treating you?" The last couple of times, he gave the honest answer. The response was the same: "Some women don't appreciate a good thing." Each time, there was a wink at the end of the statement.

Arthur was climbing his middle years, but he had plenty of lead left in the pencil.

Only got one life to live. Might as well enjoy it.

The dopamine hit from the thought solidified his decision. He would dump Wanda without losing a dime. If she tried to put up a court battle, he had a solution for that too. Luckily, he was good with accounting, and kept track of nearly every dollar of his that she spent. If he played his cards right, it would be a relatively easy and smooth divorce. Wanda would be left with nothing at the end. She would be back to square one.

Except for one thing...

That dopamine hit faded as he realized one flaw in his thinking. He would *not* be able to drop Wanda without losing a dime. In fact, the court would likely order him to pay for her lawyer fees. Knowing Wanda, she would drag the process out just to make him bleed cash. She would probably go public with allegations of abuse, which the media would run with.

Not probably... she would DEFINITELY do this. Hell, she'd do it just out of spite. That fat bitch.

Arthur watched the wedding with a bitter look on his face. Reality sank in. Wanda was bound to make his existence a living hell, whether he left her or not.

Right now, all he wanted was for this wedding to be over with so he could drown his sorrows in bourbon.

"As I guide..." The officiant paused, his attention briefly drawn to the father of the bride. A few other gazes followed, including a stern one by Leslie.

Sensing the energy in the yard swiftly changing, the officiant continued the declaration of intent, clearing his throat to save face.

"Eh-hem! Excuse me. As I guide you in exchanging your vows, you, Leslie, and you, Dale, will declare your intentions for a lasting partnership in love and marriage. Are you prepared to do this?"

"Yes," Leslie said.

"Yes," Dale said.

"Without further ado, let's begin. Dale, repeat after me: I, Dale, take you…"

Blaring sirens drew the attention of the entire congregation.

Arthur's bitter attitude was now bordering on unhinged anger. The negative energy silently directed at his freeloading maybe-soon-to-be ex-wife was now directed at the cop car pulling into his driveway.

He was the first to stand up.

"The hell is this shit?!"

"Thank God," Val said. "Everyone's here. And pissed off."

"Let them be pissed," Taylor said. There were at least fifty people seated in front of the wedding party, and all of them were looking at the new arrivals.

Taylor parked behind the last vehicle in line at the driveway, then stepped out. As she and Val approached, Arthur and Wanda were approaching, followed by a small mob.

"You!" Arthur said, pointing a finger at Val. "That's it! I've had it!"

"You guys need to get away from the water," Val said.

"You need to get the hell off my property," Wanda shouted.

"Actually, it's *my* property," Arthur abruptly said. Wanda stopped and glared at him. She had the face of someone who had a hundred different thoughts running through her head.

"What?!"

Arthur waved her off. "It's my property. I pay the bills. All you do is eat sandwiches and put on the pounds."

"You piece of shit! You're really on a roll this morning, aren't you?"

"No, because we haven't had sex this morning," Arthur said. He turned his attention to the deputy and the ex-con. "Now, get back in your vehicle and vacate immediately."

After the last twelve hours, Val and Taylor were certain they had seen it all. Nothing could leave them as flabbergasted as encountering monster crabs. They were wrong.

For a moment, they had forgotten what they had come here for. Now they, along with most of the people crowding around, were caught off guard by Arthur's seemingly random outburst at his wife.

The sheriff and three other deputies arrived.

"Excuse me, Mr. Bowen," the Sheriff said. "I'm so sorry to interrupt this event, but you need to evacuate this area immediately. Your group is in significant danger."

"What's going on?!" the bride shouted.

"I'm handling it!" Arthur replied.

"Is this a joke?! This is my wedding? Why are the police here? Why is that crazy guy here?!"

Val raised an eyebrow. *These people* were calling *him* the crazy one.

"Just hold on, Leslie," Arthur said.

She began to cry. "My wedding is ruined!"

Arthur turned around and threw his hands up and down. "Shut up, Leslie! For God's sake, you dumb little princess! You freak out about every little fucking thing! Good-fucking-luck, Dale!"

Now, Leslie was sobbing. She turned and ran to the dock, her fiancé hurrying to comfort her.

"You piece of shit!" Wanda slapped Arthur across the face. "You're a horrible human being!"

"Oh, go tumble down the hill." He chuckled. "Or, how 'bout roll down the hill. Might be faster."

Even the sheriff was standing in stunned silence. Somehow, this interaction managed to be stranger than the existence of mutated crabs. They had managed to go from being pissed about the interruption to being pissed... at each other.

Wanda slapped him again. "Like you haven't been pounding down the biscuits yourself. Asshole."

"Yeah, but I carry it well. Don't see anything hanging over my beltline."

This time, Wanda lunged at him with full force. For a woman her size, she was surprisingly spry. Like a cat, she clawed at Arthur's face. The congregation joined in.

Confusion and chaos erupted. Instead of breaking up the fight, these insane morons joined in. There was no clear distinction between alliances. People were just brawling at random.

Taylor, the sheriff, and the other deputies jumped in to intervene. A few state troopers arrived just in time for the insanity to unfold. They parked their Interceptors and joined in.

"Dispatch! We need additional backup!" the Sheriff said.

"SWAT's on the way."

"Not just them. Call every officer you can."

Val, meanwhile, had no choice but to stand aside and observe. There had to be some serious mental illness in this group. That, or they were entitled beyond belief.

The sound of a bloodcurdling scream from the lakeshore made his heart jump into his throat. He looked to the dock, half-expecting to see giant claws reaching up from the water.

Instead, it was just the bride, screaming uncontrollably, her face buried in her hands. She threw her bouquet into the water, her screaming ceasing just long enough for her to take a breath before resuming. The groom and officiant stood beside her in an attempt to comfort her.

Their attempts were met with slaps by the crazed bride.

The officiant's voice managed to echo above the melee.

Val was astonished. These people had done the impossible. For a moment, he actually forgot about mutant killer crabs in the lake.

"What the hell?!" The officiant shouted. "You know what?! To hell with you and your wedding. You're only marrying him for the money anyway!"

Now, Dale was getting heated. "The hell did you say to my wife?!"

"She's not your wife, dipshit. You haven't said the vows or been declared husband and wife! Frankly, these cops probably did you a favor by showing up all of a sudden."

"My life is ruined!" Leslie screamed.

"Evidently not," the officiant said. He pointed a finger at Dale. "Clearly this chump is willing to give you free access to his wallet in exchange for some cooch."

A second brawl ignited.

The groomsmen and numerous guests ran up to the dock. Unlike the people at the top of the hill, they at least went over there to break up the fight. They were too late, however. By the time they arrived, Dale and the officiant tumbled off the dock into the lake.

Splash!

A few boaters were on the water, watching as the madness progressed. One was a small twelve-foot aluminum boat with two guys aboard, fishing rods in hand. The other was a paddleboat with a young man and presumably his girlfriend, their romantic moment interrupted by this morning's show.

Their facial expressions mirrored Val's. For a few short moments, he had again completely forgotten about the killer crabs.

The reminder came in brutal, bloody fashion.

Leslie's next scream was one of genuine horror. The thrashing in the water intensified as giant white-tipped claws seized both men. Dale was raised over the water, clutched by the right shoulder and his groin.

He wailed, gagged, then gave a brief, but intense scream. The crab bent him backward until his spine snapped like a popsicle stick.

Behind him the officiant was pulled in every direction, the water around him turning red. Multiple pairs of pincers hacked at him, reducing him to chunks of meat.

By the time the screaming guests began their retreat, it was too late. Six more crabs, standing six feet in height with a leg-span of eleven feet, stormed the property. Maddened by hunger and radiation exposure, these crabs sought to kill anything and anyone in their vicinity.

The death toll immediately began its climb.

A scream by one of the guests was immediately cut short due to the severing of his head. His killer did not hesitate to go for the next victim. Like ants, they were interested in collecting as much food as possible before settling down to feed. It scurried over the headless corpse, quickly closing the distance on the next guest. Closing its pincers tightly, it severed the man's left leg below the knee. He fell to the grass and attempted to crawl, only to arch backward when those claws penetrated his thighs.

As he was torn apart, the other five selected their own targets. One by one, they snagged a victim, then forced him or her to the ground, where they systematically removed limbs and organs.

Leslie Bowen watched with wide eyes as people ran throughout the yard. Chairs were tossed aside, the wedding arch was knocked over, the cake table smashed and spread all over the lawn before being painted red with blood.

In her shock, she could only form one cohesive thought: *My special day is ruined.*

One of the crabs, having disemboweled one of the groomsmen, turned around and spotted her on the dock.

Leslie attempted to run, but there was nowhere to go. The entryway to the dock was cut off by the crustacean. Every other direction was covered in water. Even now, she was afraid to get her wedding dress wet.

Furry claws, almost like the arms of a bear, dragged her down. She felt the tearing of her dress, then of her flesh.

No matter how loud the screams were, Arthur Bowen and his congregation were so caught up with their brawl, they didn't notice the invasion of crabs until the discharging of firearms. State troopers and deputy sheriffs assembled at the top of the hill and blasted at the oncoming crustaceans.

Wanda, her dress torn and sagging off of her body, watched in horror.

"Oh my God! They're giant crabs! Where's Leslie? Where—OH MY GOD!"

"Get back, lady!" one of the troopers said. He had his Glock aimed downhill, trying to avoid some of the fleeing crowd. Wanda tried to break through the line, only for him to push her back. "It's too dangerous."

One of the crabs started up the hill, flinching as police gunfire struck its shell. The trooper squeezed off a few rounds, attempting to land a shot in its mouth.

"One of those things is killing my daughter!" Wanda tried harder, this time ramming the trooper at full force. The collision jarred his aim. His next shot went wide, straight into the chest of one of the groomsmen.

The poor sucker looked at the blood running down his torso, then dropped to his knees in pain. His misery was tripled as one of the crabs closed in on him. It forced him on his back, and with a single snip of its claws, it opened his belly. Coughing up blood, he watched in shock and fascination as his entrails were scooped out like fettuccine.

Wanda stood in shock, seeing the killer crab in front of her, and the massacre taking place behind it.

Taylor Davies's voice was heard over the crowd. "Arthur! Grab your wife and get her back!"

Arthur spotted Wanda on the top of the hill near the already weakening line of troopers and deputies. As the crabs closed in, several of the officers were beginning to backpedal. Being human, they were more interested in saving their own skin.

He sprinted toward his wife, palms out in front of him. "Wanda! Wanda!" There was an exaggerated quality to his voice. "Don't go, Wanda! Oh no!" His outstretched hands 'accidentally' pushed her forward.

She rolled down the hill like a barrel, straight into the grasp of the oncoming crab.

"Oh, no! Somebody save my wife!" he cried out.

The crab took advantage of the easy meal. Its claws pulled at the fat rolls, slowly peeling them off the bone. Wanda shifted left and right in a vain effort to free herself. The crab held her down, fighting against her motions, but also trying to keep her from rolling down the rest of the hill.

Two other crabs joined in. In a rare display, they dug in without fighting each other. In this instance, there was enough to share.

As the other three marched up the hill, the surviving members of the congregation retreated to their vehicles. Several cars smashed into each other during the clumsy evacuation attempt. There was no order, no regard for others, no consideration for anything except escape.

Metal vehicles ground against each other, jamming the driveway after a few short seconds. Tires scraped against gravel and pavement, horns honked, drivers screamed at each other.

The blockade impeded both the arrival of reinforcements and the attempts of law enforcement to escape.

Nearly a dozen police officers were trapped between the hill and the driveway.

"What do we do?!" one deputy shouted. "Our guns aren't stopping them!!!" As he spoke, the crabs reached the top of the hill. Their white pincers, now stained red, yawned open.

The Sheriff did not have an answer. All he could think to say was "RUN!"

Officers ran in all directions, several immediately falling to the crustaceans. They were amazingly swift for their size, and with immeasurable strength, they ripped their victims apart.

After a few minutes, the three that fed on Wanda decided to join the fray. Some officers ran through the tree line on the sides of the property. One tripped over the orange extension cable and face-planted in the grass. His attempt to crawl away was brief.

Pincers pierced his back and closed over his spine, by which the crab lifted him off the ground. Holding his spinal cord like a briefcase handle, it picked at him with its other pincer.

Val backed up to the house, looking for Taylor amid the chaos.

"Taylor!"

"Val!"

She ran to him, pistol in hand. Already, the spare ammunition she had taken from the SUV had nearly been used up. Only a few bullets remained.

They caught their breath by the garage, then looked to the sound of screaming coming from the front entrance. The DJs were at the door, yelling at Arthur Bowen who had locked it from the inside.

"LET US IN! LET US IN!" They turned around and threw their hands over their eyes as a crab burst through the small patio fence. It grabbed the DJ with the weird mustache by the throat and lifted him in the same manner as a comic book villain. The DJ squirmed, then went limp following the cracking of his neck. The other one tried to run, only to trip on one of the lounge chairs. The crab tossed the dead victim aside in favor of the live one.

"OH GOD! OH NO! HEEEELLLLP MEEE!!!!"

It flayed him open and pulled his kidneys out, which it ate like lima beans.

By now, Taylor was numb to the whole bloodshed.

"I had no idea there were this many of them," Val said. "Unless we order a freaking air strike, I have no idea how we're gonna stop them... Wait a minute..."

Taylor backed away, pointing her pistol at the crab on the patio. After killing the DJ, it began moving toward them.

"Don't have a minute!"

"This way." Val led her around the garage to the back entrance. As luck would have it, it was locked. Arthur had probably gone through the house and locked it in hopes the crabs would be distracted with all of the people outside.

Val stood out of the way, gesturing to Taylor's pistol and the door handle.

"Mind doing the honors?"

She put a few rounds through the latch then kicked the door open. Val went inside and immediately started searching along the walls.

"Not sure hiding in here will work," Taylor said.

"That's not the plan," Val said. "We're going to trap them and   gas   them."
"Gas them with what?"

"With—AH-HA! Here they are!" He rushed to the back corner, where Arthur kept his Cardinal backpack mosquito sprayers and the jugs of pesticides. He picked one of the packs up, then squeezed the nozzle trigger to test it. A white cloud of poison mist drifted out. "Perfect. If we can get these bastards through the garage door, we can lure then in, then shut it behind them."

"Then unload the foggers," Taylor said. She looked to one of the shelves. As luck would have it, Mr. Bowen had a full can of wasp spray in stock. She snatched it up and shook it. "If we make it out of this, I might have to buy a stock in whatever company makes this stuff."

"You and I both," Val replied.

"We can use a car to barricade the hinge door," Taylor said. "You sure these walls can contain them? We saw they were able to rip through your house."

"It'll hold them long enough," Val said. "If they breach, we'll use the wasp spray to keep them inside and use duct tape to keep the gas from escaping." He grabbed a roll of tape off the wall and tucked it under his arm.

Another scream from outside ended the debate.

Taylor ran to the garage door control. "Might as well try." She pressed the top button, lifting the front overhead doors.

The lawn came into view, as did four of the crabs. The one that was on the patio had moved to the left, joining another in

174

an effort to pin down the Sheriff. He backed toward the woods, firing the last few rounds in his pistol.

Taylor jumped up and down, swinging her hands wildly. "Sheriff!" He looked past the crabs in her direction. "Sheriff! Bring them over here! Get them into the damn garage!"

No questions were asked. The Sheriff ran wide of the crab, narrowly dodging its snapping claws. The crustaceans rotated in place, then followed him to the house.

Taylor proceeded to yell at the other officers in front of the building.

"Bring them HERE! Hurry!"

Emptying their guns into the crustaceans, the cops relayed the order and began assembling near the garage.

All six crabs converged.

"I sure hope you have a plan!" the Sheriff said.

"Get outside," Taylor said.

"Hurry!" Val added. "Out the back way. Someone get a car and block this door once we're out."

The Sheriff saw the jugs of pesticide at the contractor's feet, then quickly understood the plan. Like a drill instructor, he ushered the other cops through the garage.

Taylor stood at the controls, waiting for the crabs to get close enough so she could press the button and have the door close while they entered the garage.

"Wait!" the Sheriff said. "If I may... it's best to leave this door open, then circle around, toss the sprayers through the front door. Here..." He yanked on the emergency release cord, allowing the door to be shut manually.

The crabs were right there. Like a group of rioters, they swarmed into the garage.

For the second time, the Sheriff jumped back, narrowly avoiding the reach of snapping claws.

"GO! GO! FUCKING GO!"

Val was out the door, then Taylor, then the sheriff, who happily slammed it shut.

A heavy impact struck the inside, nearly knocking him backward. Val joined him in the effort to keep the door shut.

Taylor ran to the blockade of vehicles, choosing a pickup truck.

"I need to borrow this vehicle," she said to the driver.

"Go to hell!"

She put her gun to the window. "Who do you fear more? The crabs? Or *me*?"

The driver swallowed, then exited the vehicle.

She got in and brought it over to the back door. Val and the Sheriff stepped aside, allowing her to line it up. Taylor parked the truck outside the door, then stepped out.

The crabs struck the door, the mass of the vehicle successfully keeping it shut. They struck again, this time with enough force to splinter it.

"Hurry!" the Sheriff said.

Val grabbed the packs and followed him and Taylor to the garage door. They stopped at the corner, just out of sight. Using the duct tape he stole from the garage, Val depressed the nozzle triggers.

White clouds pumped from the muzzles.

"Here. Take a whiff!" He threw the sprayers into the garage. The crabs turned around, momentarily confused by the rumbling devices spewing the gassy substance.

Val grabbed the garage door and pulled it down, trapping them inside.

A heavy hit shook the whole door.

"Shit!" he exclaimed, jumping away.

The door reverberated as a dozen claws drummed against it.

"They're trapped inside!" one of the troopers shouted. A set of pincers penetrated the door. "WHOA!"

"Hang on! I anticipated this," Val said. Shaking his can of wasp spray, he approached the breach. He waited for the claw to withdraw, then fired a foamy stream through the breach.

The chemical hit its mark, sending the crab into an even bigger frenzy. Feverish and confused, the crab retreated to the inner wall, where it began tearing down all the tools.

Val fired a few more streams, effectively driving the crabs away from the garage door. He tossed the can to Taylor, freeing his hands so he could efficiently place duct tape over the breach to keep the mosquito spray trapped.

They could hear the sprayers doing their work. Thin mist escaped under the bottom of the door, indicating the inside was one giant chemical cloud.

"It's working," Taylor said.

The anarchy intensified. There was a nonstop sound of snapping claws and thrashing about. Tools, electrical conduits, and shelves were torn from the walls. The entire house shook, as a new melee took place.

A melee between crazed, chemical-ridden crabs.

Arthur Bowen was inside his bedroom, crouched near his closet. He held a .357 snub-nosed revolver in one hand and a bottle of bourbon in the other. For a while, it appeared he would only have to focus on one rather than the other. The crabs were busy with the snacks outside, after all. If any good came from this, he would never have to share this lake house ever again.

Better yet, he didn't even have to worry about the time it would take divorcing Wanda. These giant crabs were a blessing in disguise. When choosing a new partner, he would not only have his finances to rely on, but the fact that he was a widower. Perhaps he would enjoy several rounds of sympathy sex before he settled down again.

Only now was it starting to dawn on him that his daughter had been killed by the things. He did not hold the same disdain for her as he did his wife, though Leslie did irritate him to the max. Probably it was the fact that she was his daughter, which inevitably meant she would marry off and be someone else's problem. Namely Dale, who was nowhere to be seen during the mayhem.

The sound of snapping claws and destruction sounded closer. The house was shaking from nonstop impacts. A huge collective mass acted as a whirlwind, threatening to lift the house up by the roots.

Arthur put his hand to the floor and felt the rumblings. Were they in the garage?!

He cut through the house, arriving at the garage interior door. He opened it a crack and peered through.

What he saw was a storm of mosquito spray, teeming with black, crustacean bodies.

"JESUS CHRIST!!!"

Some jackass trapped the crabs in the garage.

There was no way in hell Arthur was going to wait inside and let these things tear through the walls. With the driveway jammed, he needed a different escape route.

He went to the front door to look at the lawn. The path was clear, save for the assemblage of dismembered corpses. His boat was still moored on his dock. All he had to do was sprint and go for it.

That was exactly what he did.

"What the—" Val watched with the same fascination as the police officers as Arthur Bowen raced down to the dock on the right. He ran with the speed of an Olympic runner, arriving at his boat in less than fifteen seconds. He removed the mooring lines and backed the boat up with his oars. Once he was clear of the dock, he started the motor and turned the boat around.

Off he went, southbound into the interior of the lake. Not once did he look back.

The group turned their attention back to the garage door.

Slowly, but truly, the ruckus inside began to slow. The battering of walls became less intense, the clattering of rock-hard legs against the concrete floor less frequent.

There were wet sounds now, as though the crabs were vomiting.

The battering soon reduced to tapping, the tapping to grazing, the grazing to silence.

Val did not dare to open the garage door for several more minutes. By then, backup had arrived, including SWAT. Officers and EMT's swarmed the property on foot, each responder visually disturbed by the hellish landscape that was now the Bowen property.

"What happened?" the SWAT commander said.

Several more moments of silence passed.

The Sheriff nodded to Val, who slowly lifted the door a few inches. Hearing no signs of an escape attempt, he lifted it the rest of the way.

The fog parted and escaped into the atmosphere, unveiling the six suffocated Chinese mitten crabs inside. A few of them twitched. It was nothing more than minor muscle spasms. They were as dead as the people on the lawn.

"*That* happened," the Sheriff replied.

CHAPTER 24

The next several hours were spent giving statements to the media and to the National Guard, which had been deployed at the request of the local government. The entire lake had been sealed off, with all residences evacuated. Soon, air patrols would sweep the lake repeatedly in search of any straggling boaters, and boat units would comb the lake for any remaining crabs.

It was six in the afternoon when Val and Taylor managed to get out of there. Afterward, they went to Val's house so he could collect a few personal items.

Taylor steered the dented-up SUV into his driveway. The officers who were monitoring the scene had been called to assist at the Bowen property, leaving the place eerily vacant. There were still blood stains in the grass. The lawn was swarming with hungry insects eager to get whatever scraps they could.

"Still thinking of staying?" Taylor said.

"Starting to rethink that, unfortunately," Val said. "Hard to say. I like to think that this lake will get cleaned up in the coming months. I have to remain optimistic." He noticed a small smile on the deputy's face. "What?"

"I just like your attitude," she said.

"Well, it got me through prison. It got me where I am today. I can tell you, my uncle would be rolling in his grave if I started feeling sorry for myself now." He stepped out of the SUV and went for his door. "Hopefully, those crabs didn't go through my clothes during the night."

"I have a feeling they're safe," Taylor said.

Val took a moment to look at the building. There was so much damage done by the crabs, cleaning up seemed overwhelming. It almost seemed it would be simpler to just tear the house down and rebuild from scratch.

He took his own advice and refused to let it bring him down. It was easier said than done, but strength of character was necessary to persevere in life. He would get through this hard chapter, for he knew great things lay ahead.

"Hey, uh…" Taylor stepped out of the vehicle and caught up with him.

"Yeah?"

"You… need anywhere to stay?"

"Was kinda working on that," he said. "I've got money for a hotel."

"Frequent hotel stays are gonna get expensive," she said. "And, no offense, but it doesn't look like you'll be working for a week or so."

Val looked at his damaged truck. "Probably not."

"Listen…" she nervously ruffled some stones under her boot. "I, uh, have a spare room. If, you know, you needed a place to stay."

A spark of anxiety struck Val. It was a generous offer, one that he felt he should be gentlemen enough to turn down. A man and woman under the same roof? He worried it was inappropriate. It wasn't as though they were an item.

Or is this her way of changing that?

Yet turning down the offer felt wrong. He never made a point to admire her figure—though she had a good one—but rather he always noticed her kind treatment of him. Being in her company would be better than staying in a dull, empty hotel room for God knows how long.

"Oh, that's alright," he said. "I wouldn't want to intrude."

"No, it's alright," she said. "I got a decent-sized place. There's plenty of room. You can stay there until you get back on your feet. You deserve it. I mean, you did save my ass like a hundred times in the last twenty hours."

Val smiled.

"You sure it's alright?"

"Absolutely."

"Okay." He nodded in appreciation. "Thank you, Taylor."

She smiled back at him. "You're welcome."

"OH MY GOD!!!" It was a sound of grotesque horror, coming from the neighbor's house. "OH MY GOD! JESUS CHRIST! HOLY SHIT!!! WHAT IN THE NAME OF—"

Val and Taylor ran through the woods. Taylor reached for her radio mic, ready to call for backup to rescue whoever was getting attacked.

They got through the trees, then stopped. There were no crabs, aside from the dead ones.

Standing in the driveway was Charles Netty. With an open jaw and his hands clasped behind his head, he looked at the path of destruction that was his property. His car's engine was still running, not even having reached the end of the driveway.

After gazing at the ravaged house, charred lawn, and monster corpses, he turned his eyes to Val.

"Wha—wha—WHAT HAPPENED?!?!"

Val smiled nervously, gesturing at the devastation before him.

"Well... I did tell ya when you left, didn't I? 'When you get back, the cable trench won't even be on your mind.'"

CHAPTER 25

The cove was dark and wet. The overhanging branches kept him obscured from the choppers flying overhead. Hearing the motors gave the impression that the threat at the house had been dealt with. These were not just police and news choppers. There were military aircraft flying about as well, probably in search of other crabs.

Arthur Bowen remained crouched on the back seat of his boat, sipping on his bottle of bourbon. His drunken mind was battered by conflicting thoughts. He was grateful to be absolved of Wanda's nonstop leeching and nagging. His finances would undoubtedly improve over this life change.

However, it was finally dawning on him that Leslie was dead too. The poor kid was annoying as hell, and like her mother, was pretty much a walking drainage pipe for his bank account. Still, she did not deserve what happened to her.

On the other hand, it wasn't as though no good came from this. While crouched in the cove, he was able to find a hotspot to connect to the internet with his phone. There were countless reports about the incident. More importantly, there were reports of radioactivity detected in the creek on the south end of the lake.

Arthur wasn't an expert on nuclear contamination, but it was simple math to figure out the giant crabs and radioactivity were related.

With that knowledge came the plus side. He would be able to sue the plant responsible for millions. Hell, considering that he lost a wife *and* a kid to the crabs, he could probably get tens of millions if not hundreds. Being an experienced attorney, he knew exactly how he would plan the case. It was a guaranteed win. Even in a settlement, they would pay so much, Arthur would never have to bother with lawyering ever again.

"I can just go fly fishing, go boating, fly to Europe and Cancun whenever I want...fucking anything!" He grinned. "Damn. These crabs really were a blessing in disguise."

A warm feeling came over him, and it wasn't the summer weather. All he had to do now was go back and play the role of the distraught husband and father. The booze on his breath would help with the authenticity of his performance. News cameras were probably still at his house, which would help set the stage for his lawsuit.

First thing's first, he had to pull up the anchor. He leaned over the stern and tugged on the rope. He strained, barely able to raise it a few inches. The damn thing was way heavier than he expected it to be. Either it was caught in mud or weeds, or he was really out of shape.

He shifted into a better position, then tugged with all of his might. Straining, he finally made some progress. The weight did not alleviate as he hoisted the big block of concrete.

A big blob breached the surface. A vile smell instantly struck Arthur, nearly causing him to lose his grip on the rope. He swung it over the edge of the boat and let it drop. A loud metal *clang* shook the small vessel.

"What in the hell?"

The anchor was completely encased in a strange gooey substance. Weeds, silt, baby bluegills, and small crayfish were trapped in this ball of slime like flies in a spiderweb.

Arthur waved his hand in an attempt to brush the smell away.

"Good lord. What the hell is this crap?"

He lifted the anchor and shook it a few times. The stuff simply dangled, its tight grasp withstanding his efforts.

It didn't matter. It was only slime.

Arthur yanked on the motor cord. The propellor spun, then died. He yanked again.

"Come on, you piece of shit."

He yanked again.

THUMP!

Arthur fell against the rear of the boat, catching himself on the prop. That smell intensified to the point where he could nearly taste it.

There was a sound of dripping water behind him. Tremors of motion traveled through the boat, whose bow was now mysteriously tipping down. Hearing the wet sticky sound,

Arthur hesitated. He felt a presence watching him from the front seat.

He did not want to look. Yet, oddly, *not* looking was somehow worse.

Maybe it's nothing. Maybe it's just the bourbon having gone to your head. Can't be a crab. You'd hear the legs and claws grabbing the boat.

He turned around.

He wished he hadn't. It was like looking at the face of a horrible executioner. In his case, the executioner had no eyes. Its fat greenish-yellow body, layered with wet, leathery skin, oozed a saliva substance which helped it to cling to the hull. Its rounded head was poised like a cobra's.

The skin at its center rippled, then peeled back. Three pairs of jaws, like green flower petals lined with triangular teeth, dripped water and slime.

"Oh…"

He downed the rest of his bottle in a few fast gulps.

First giant crabs. Now a giant leech?!

The creature lunged, constricting around Arthur's body before piercing him with its jaws. The shift in weight flipped the boat, sending both of them into the water.

Arthur gagged, feeling his bodily fluids sucked out through the wound. It was a fast, yet agonizing process. His eyes shriveled into the back of their sockets like deflated balloons. His mouth stretched, his cheeks hugging the jawline as every drop of blood was rapidly drained.

Thirty seconds later, the leech finished. Now fat and satiated, it swam off, leaving a skeletal husk at the bottom of the cove.

No longer did Arthur Bowen have to worry about his bank account being sucked dry.

THE END

Check out other great

Sea Monster Novels!

Michael Cole

SCAR

Scar is a killing machine. Born from DNA spliced between the extinct Megalodon and modern day Great White, he has a viciousness that transcends time. His evil is reflected in his eyes, his savagery in his two-inch serrated teeth, his ruthlessness in his trail of death. After escaping captivity, the killer shark travels to the island community Cross Point, where prey is in abundance. With an insatiable appetite, heightened senses, and skin impervious to bullets, Scar kills everything that crosses his path. His reign of terror puts him at war with the island sheriff, Nick Piatt. With the body count rising, Nick vows to protect his island community from the vicious threat. With the aid of a marine biologist, a rookie deputy, and a bad-tempered fisherman, Nick leads a crusade against Scar, as well as the ruthless scientist who created him.

Rick Chesler

HOTEL MEGALODON

An underwater luxury hotel on a gorgeous tropical island is set for an extravagant opening weekend with the world watching. The only thing standing in the way of a first-rate experience for the jet-setting VIPs is an unscrupulous businessman and sixty feet of prehistoric shark. As the underwater complex is besieged by a marauding behemoth, newly minted marine biologist Coco Keahi must face off against the ancient predator as it rises from the deep with a vengeance. Meanwhile, a human monster has decided he would be better off if Coco were one of the creature's victims.

Check out other great

Sea Monster Novels!

Matt James

SUB-ZERO

The only thing colder than the Antarctic air is the icy chill of death... Off the coast of McMurdo Station, in the frigid waters of the Southern Ocean, a new species of Antarctic octopus is unintentionally discovered. Specialists aboard a state-of-the-art DARPA research vessel aim to apply the animal's "sub-zero venom" to one of their projects: An experimental painkiller designed for soldiers on the front lines. All is going according to plan until the ship is caught in an intense storm. The retrofitted tanker is rocked, and the onboard laboratory is destroyed. Amid the chaos, the lead scientist is infected by a strange virus while conducting the specimen's dissection. The scientist didn't die in the accident. He changed.

Alister Hodge

THE CAVERN

When a sink hole opens up near the Australian outback town of Pintalba, it uncovers a pristine cave system. Sam joins an expedition to explore the subterranean passages as paramedic support, hoping to remain unneeded at base camp. But, when one of the cavers is injured, he must overcome paralysing claustrophobia to dive pitch-black waters and squeeze through the bowels of the earth. Soon he will find there are fates worse than being buried alive, for in the abandoned mines and caves beneath Pintalba, there are ravenous teeth in the dark. As a savage predator targets the group with hideous ferocity, Sam and his friends must fight for their lives if they are ever to see the sun again.

Check out other great

Sea Monster Novels!

Michael Cole

CREATURE OF LAKE SHADOW

It was supposed to be a simple bank robbery. Quick. Clean. Efficient. It was none of those. With police searching for them across the state, a band of criminals hide out in a desolate cabin on the frozen shore of Lake Shadow. Isolated, shrouded in thick forest, and haunted by a mysterious history, they thought it was the perfect place to hide. Tensions mount as they hear strange noises outside. Slain animals are found in the snow. Before long, they realize something is watching them. Something hungry, violent, and not of this world. In their attempt to escape, they found the Creature of Lake Shadow.

C.J. Waller

PREDATOR X

When deep level oil fracking uncovers a vast subterranean sea, a crack team of cavers and scientists are sent down to investigate. Upon their arrival, they disappear without a trace. A second team, including sedimentologist Dr Megan Stoker, are ordered to seek out Alpha Team and report back their findings. But Alpha team are nowhere to be found – instead, they are faced with something unexpected in the depths. Something ancient. Something huge. Something dangerous. Predator X

Printed in Great Britain
by Amazon

19097742R00108